Francis G. B. Northbrook, Thomas Baring, William H. J. Weale

A Descriptive Catalogue

Of the Collection of Pictures Belonging to the Earl of Northbrook

Francis G. B. Northbrook, Thomas Baring, William H. J. Weale

A Descriptive Catalogue
Of the Collection of Pictures Belonging to the Earl of Northbrook

ISBN/EAN: 9783337142261

Printed in Europe, USA, Canada, Australia, Japan

Cover: Foto ©Andreas Hilbeck / pixelio.de

More available books at **www.hansebooks.com**

DESCRIPTIVE CATALOGUE.

Thomas Baring.

*A DESCRIPTIVE CATALOGUE OF
THE COLLECTION OF PICTURES
BELONGING TO THE EARL OF
NORTHBROOK.*

THE DUTCH, FLEMISH, AND FRENCH SCHOOLS
BY MR. W. H. JAMES WEALE; THE ITALIAN
AND SPANISH SCHOOLS BY DR. JEAN PAUL
RICHTER.

WITH TWENTY-FIVE ILLUSTRATIONS — PHOTOGRAPHS BY
HENRY DIXON & SON, BY THE DIXON AND GRAY ORTHO-
CHROMATIC PROCESS, PRINTED IN PLATINOTYPE.

LONDON: GRIFFITH, FARRAN, OKEDEN & WELSH.
AND SYDNEY.
1889.

HENRY SOTHERAN & Co.
Booksellers,
— AND —
Bookbinders.
ESTABLISHED 1816.

BY APPOINTMENT

TO
H.R.H. THE PRINCE OF WALES.

Telegraphic Address – BOOKMEN. LONDON
CODE IN USE UNICODE.

37, PICCADILLY, W.
NEAR THE ROYAL ACADEMY.

PUBLISHERS OF MR GOULD'S GRAND ORNITHOLOGICAL WORKS.

CONTENTS.

—+—

EXPLANATION OF REFERENCES.

— ** —

In the descriptions of the pictures the dimensions are given in inches, the first measurement indicating the height, the second the width of the canvas or panel without the frame. The terms "right" and "left" denote the right and left of the picture, as seen by the spectator standing in front of it.

The price has been given when the pictures have been bought or sold by public auction. In recent years the sales were almost all at Christie's.

A list of the works to which reference is made in the descriptions will be found in Appendix III.

INTRODUCTION.

The Collection of Pictures described in this Catalogue was, with very few exceptions, made by the late Mr. Thomas Baring, who bequeathed it to his nephew, Lord Northbrook.

Mr. Thomas Baring was the second son of Sir Thomas Baring, and brother of Francis Thornhill Baring, first Lord Northbrook. He had been brought up in familiarity with good pictures, for his grandfather, Sir Francis Baring, acquired a fine collection of Dutch masters at the end of the last century. On the death of Sir Francis in 1810 his son, Sir Thomas, parted with the Dutch collection to the Prince Regent, and formed a gallery mainly composed of Italian pictures.[*] Afterwards he added to it some works by English and Dutch masters.

Mr. Baring began his collection in 1835, and constantly added to it till 1871, two years before he died. He kept a careful account of his purchases, from which the particulars given in this Catalogue have been principally taken.

In 1846, Mr. Baring, Mr. Jones Loyd (the late Lord

---

[*] The commencement of this collection was made by the purchase of a number of pictures collected by M. Le Brun in 1808. A list of them will be found in Appendix II.

Overstone), and the late Mr. Humphrey Mildmay, bought
the collection of Dutch pictures of Baron Verstolk van
Soelen, of the Hague, who died in that year. Among
Mr. Baring's papers there is a complete list of this important collection, which is printed in Appendix I. In 1848,
on the death of Sir Thomas Baring, his collection was
sold in accordance with his will; and the Italian, Spanish,
and French pictures were bought at a valuation by Mr.
Baring. These pictures are noted in the Catalogue as from
Sir Thomas Baring's collection.

N.

ILLUSTRATIONS.

EARLY NETHERLANDISH SCHOOL.

1   1. VIRGIN AND CHILD ENTHRONED.

Panel, oak. 5¼ × 4 in. Figure 3 in.

The Virgin, seated facing the spectator, wears a greenish blue dress lined with grey fur. On her head is a magnificent floriated crown, richly set with rubies, sapphires, and pearls, from beneath which her long fair hair falls in masses over her shoulders. With her right hand she supports the Child, while with her left she offers him the breast. His dress is red, of two shades, the pattern being darker than the ground; a little linen is shown at the neck.

The porch of stone in which they are enthroned is richly adorned with sculpture, the interior of the arch has delicate open-work cusps. The statues on the pediments represent three prophets with scrolls: Abraham holding a sacrificial knife, David with the harp, and Melchisedech with bread. Above the arch, in canopied niches, are groups representing the Seven Joys of the Virgin: the Annunciation, the Visitation, the Nativity, the Adoration of the Magi, the Resurrection, the Descent of the Holy Ghost at Pentecost, and the Coronation.

At the foot of the wall, on either side of the porch, are plants in flower: a columbine, an iris, a lily, &c.

This is a little gem of wonderful delicacy, painted with much body of well-blended colour, and with a precision that cannot be surpassed. The architecture, of silvery grey tone, forms an admirable setting to the rich jewel-like figure of the Virgin.

Ascribed to Van Eyck and to Memline, this picture is certainly by neither of those artists. It may with much more probability be assigned to the unknown master who executed for the Cistercian Abbey of the Dunes, near Nieuport, the diptych now in the Museum at Antwerp.

Collections—Frederick II., King of Prussia, where it was catalogued as by Albert Dürer. Sold at Paris to [?]
Mr. Aders.
Mr. Samuel Rogers.
Bought May 2, 1856, No. 585, £207, 15s.
Passavant, i. 211.
Waagen, *Treasures*, ii. 78.
Exhibited—British Institution, 1848, No. 76.

2   2. SAINT GILES.

Shutter of an altar-piece, oak.   24¼ × 18¼ in.

On the right, St. Giles, a grey-bearded hermit in a black-hooded habit and grey mantle, sits on a bank. His right hand, transfixed by an arrow, rests on the back of a fawn which has fled to him for protection. On the left is the hunting-party, the leader of which, kneeling on one knee, is begging the Saint's pardon. He wears a dark lilac dress and greenish-blue surcoat, lined with red and gold brocade, a black cap, and untanned hunting-boots. Beside him kneels a priest (perhaps the donor of the altar-piece) in red furred cassock and surplice, with a blue almuce over his shoulders. In the foreground, to the left, stands a young man (probably the painter) in green, with a crimson cloak which he holds up with his right hand ; on his head a black cap. Behind is a group of four youths, the archer who has shot the fatal arrow, and five mounted attendants.

The foreground consists of a variety of flowers ; iris, great mullen, &c., most delicately painted. Behind St. Giles are some rocks, at the foot of which is a hermit's cell with a crucifix ; from the rock gushes forth a spring of water, near which is a youth holding a couple of hounds. In the middle is an elm-tree, and on the left a town with a handsome Romanesque church, a Gothic castle, and other buildings. Beyond are hills.

(2)

On the exterior of the panel, painted in grisaille, is the figure of a saint in cope and mitre, blessing, and holding a pastoral staff in his left hand.*

Formerly ascribed to Jan van Eyck and to Lucas van Leyden.

Collection—Mr. Thomas Emerson. Sold May 27, 1854, No. 63, £51, 9s., to Mr. Webb.
Bought from Mr. Webb, 1854.
Exhibited—Royal Academy, 1872, No. 224.
Photographed, *Northbrook Gallery.*

3   3. SAINTS CECILY, MARGARET, AGATHA,
AND DOROTHY.

Two panels, oak, in one frame. $13\frac{3}{4} \times 8\frac{3}{4}$ in.

The Saints are seated in a garden on a raised bank, on which are flowers in pots, a peacock and peahen, and two parrakeets. The garden is enclosed by a trellis-work fence, beyond which are a roadway and four mansions with corby-stepped gables ; on the roof of one of them is a stork's nest. The background is occupied by hills with two castles in the distance. St. Cecily, in lilac brocade with ermine lining, has an organ in her left hand and a falcon on her right. St. Margaret wears a crimson dress lined with brown fur ; she holds two white pinks, and is raising her right hand to make the sign of the cross over the dragon which lies vanquished at her feet. St. Agatha, in a scarlet dress trimmed with white fur, holds up a pair of pincers with her breast. St. Dorothy, in violet, has a sword in her right and a flower in her left hand.

Ascribed to Hans Memlinc and to Gerard van der Meire.†

Collection—Chevalier de Coninck de Merckem, Ghent. Sold August 4, 1856, 770 frs., to M. Nieuwenhuys.
Bought from M. Nieuwenhuys, 1856.

* It is not known where the centre of the altar-piece now is, but the other shutter, representing an angel with a scroll appearing to Saint Giles while saying Mass, is in the possession of the Earl of Dudley. The building in which the incident is represented as taking place is a faithful representation of the interior of the Abbey Church of St. Denys, near Paris. Engraved in Viollet-le-duc, *Dictionnaire raisonné de l'Architecture Française du xi' au xvi' Siècle,* tom. II. p. 26.
† A similar picture was, in 1860, in the possession of the Rev. Mr. Heath, Vicar of Enfield.

(3)

4   4. VIRGIN AND CHILD.

Panel, oak. $22\frac{1}{4} \times 16\frac{1}{2}$ in.

The Virgin sits in a stone alcove in a pensive attitude, holding the Child with her right arm, and resting her left on the ledge of the seat. The Child is caressing his Mother's chin with his right hand and has his left arm round her neck.

She wears a crimson dress with a green kerchief across the shoulders, and a lilac mantle, which she is gathering up with her left hand. Her wavy light hair falls down her back. The Child has light curly hair; his lower limbs are wrapped in transparent muslin. The stone alcove is ornamented with rams' heads, arabesque sculpture, and coloured marbles. The floor is a rich marble tesselated pavement.

In a very good state of preservation, this panel, painted in bright harmonious tints, dates from about the year 1515.

Formerly ascribed to Hans Memline and to Jan Gossaert (Mabuse), this picture is probably by the Master of the Mater Dolorosa in the Church of Notre Dame at Bruges.

Bought from Mr. Smith, 1851.
Waagen, *Treasures*, ii. 182.
Weale, *Bruges et ses Environs*, 4ᵉ édition, Bruges, 1882, p. 116.
Photographed, *Northbrook Gallery.*

5   5. VISION OF SAINT ILDEPHONSUS.

Panel, oak,   17¾ × 13½ in.

The Virgin appearing to St. Ildephonsus, Bishop of Toledo, after he
had by his writings and sermons refuted the heresy of Helvidius,
who had denied her virginity.

The Saint, in a girded and apparelled alb, with the maniple on his
arm, kneels on the foot-pace of an altar on the north side of a large
church of picturesque architecture, in which Gothic and Renaissance
details are mixed, the latter prevailing. He is looking up with
outstretched hands, in an ecstasy of joy, at the Virgin, who appears
on the left, attended by three angels, and is about to vest him with
a red chasuble with gold orphreys. Behind the Saint, to the right,
kneel three monks, one holding an open book, the second looking up
at the vision, and the third absorbed in prayer. In the background
is a procession of monks chanting, headed by a cross-bearer in an alb.

This richly-coloured picture is in a good state of preservation ; the
heads of the figures in the foreground are remarkable for the sweet-
ness of their expression and the delicacy of their modelling.*

Bought from M. Nieuwenhuys, 1856, as by Van Orley.
Exhibited—Royal Academy, 1872, No. 242.

---

* A similar picture was, in 1860, in the collection of the Rev. Mr. Heath, Vicar of
Enfield.

6

6. ECCE HOMO.

Panel. 17½ × 13 in.

In the foreground our Lord is seen taking leave of his Mother, who has fallen back, supported by one of the Marys; farther to the right stands another, whilst Mary Magdalene kneels on the extreme left. On the right are St. Peter, St. John, and two other Apostles. In the middle distance, Pilate, standing, with a long white thorny wand in his hand, on a raised terrace behind a bar, shows to the people our Lord crowned with thorns, clad in a white mantle, which two men hold up, exposing to view his body torn with stripes. The people below are shouting, and vehemently demanding his crucifixion. On the wall of Pilate's house are the words *Ecce Homo*.

In the background are the buildings of a town, painted with great detail, and numerous figures; in the distance, on the right, rocks and dark clouds; on the left light is breaking.

This picture has been ascribed to Cornelius Engelbrechtsen and to Lucas van Leyden.

Collection—Mr. Thomas Baring. *
Exhibited—Royal Academy, 1880, No. 235.

---

* This description is given in those cases where, although the picture formed part of Mr. Baring's collection, I have been unable to find the date of the purchase.

7

7. FLIGHT INTO EGYPT.

Panel. 13 × 19⅜ in.

The Virgin, seated, supports with both hands the Child sitting on the back of a sheep lying on the grass. On the right Joseph leans on a staff. This group is copied from the picture by Raphael in the Museum of Madrid. The figures have outline nimbs in gold, and the borders of their garments are adorned with gilding.

The elaborately-painted landscape is traversed by a winding stream; in the foreground, on the right, is a tree with two lizards on the trunk; at its foot are rabbits, birds, butterflies, and flowers. On the river is a ferry-boat, which is nearing the farther bank, towards which the Virgin, on an ass, and Joseph are hastening. Beyond there is a group of buildings, with a village cross and soldiers; farther off, a horseman with hounds. In the background are towns and distant hills.

This picture has been ascribed to Giovanni F. Penni, but is certainly the work of a German or Fleming.

Collection—Sir Thomas Baring.
Exhibited—British Institution, 1841, No. 21.
Waagen, *Treasures*, ii, 176.

8

8. VIRGIN AND CHILD.

Panel. 14½ × 9¾ in.

The Virgin, three-quarter length, seated, supports with her right hand the Infant on a white cloth, and holds with her left the back of a book, with the leaves of which he is playing. She wears a blue dress gathered in at the neck, the sleeves lined with fur. Over her light brown hair is thrown a fine cambric veil, hidden at the back beneath a greyish-blue mantle with a gold-broidered border. Behind hangs a bluish-green cloth of honour with a murry border. On the left stands a carved wooden aumbrye with a latten candlestick on the top of it.

This picture is the work of a contemporary of Jan Gossaert.

Collections—Mr. J. P. Weyer, Cologne. Sold August 25, 1869, No. 259.
121 thalers.
Rev. James Heath.
Bought by the Earl of Northbrook, April 10, 1880, No. 148, £23, 2s.

EARLY GERMAN SCHOOL.

9

1. VIRGIN AND CHILD.

Panel, oak. 17 × 11½ in.

The Virgin and Child, half-length, on a gold crescent moon, on reddish-brown background relieved by small lines of gold. The Virgin has a tight-sleeved gold brocade dress, and a blue mantle with gold-embroidered border. Her long hair is confined by a band adorned with pearls. She supports with both hands the Child in a semi-recumbent position on a linen cloth.

Formerly ascribed to H. Aldegrever.

Collection—Mr. Thomas Baring.

10   2. INFANT CHRIST ENTHRONED.

Panel. 21¼ × 14⅝ in.

On a rich throne of brass, with crystal columns and a pierced
architectural dorsal of mixed Flamboyant and Renaissance detail, are
seated St. Anne and the Virgin, with the Infant Saviour standing
between them. He holds his Mother's mantle with his left hand,
while he extends his right to take a pink which St. Anne is offering him. Over his head broods the Holy Spirit in the form of a
dove, surrounded by a glow of yellow light; from the sky above
golden rays are shooting downwards. St. Anne wears a green
dress and a scarlet mantle, and a pink turban on a white kerchief.
A large book lies open on her lap. The Virgin, crowned, has a loose
light-blue dress and mantle, and holds an open book on her left arm.
Above hover two angels with musical instruments. On the left and
right Joachim, in a blue robe and scarlet head-covering, and Joseph,
in green with a red mantle, lean on the two arms of the throne. In
the foreground, on the left, is St. Bernard, kneeling with his hands
joined; his abbatial staff with its veil resting against his right shoulder.
Above him, on a scroll: *Monstra te esse Matrem.* In front of him,
nearer the middle, kneels the donor, in plaited shirt, scarlet dress,
and a bluish-grey furred robe with loose sleeves; in his hands is a
scarlet cap, and on the ground before him an open book. On the
right stands St. Katherine, in a cloth of gold skirt with ermine
body and border, and an enormous turban head-dress with a crown.
She holds an open book on her right arm, a sword in her left hand,
and has her foot on the prostrate figure of Maxentius, who holds a
sceptre in his left hand. In the foreground are white lilies and other
flowers. Landscape background; on the left are a stag, three old
men conversing, angels and men on a road leading through a forest
to a temple on a height in the distance, before the entrance of which
stands an angel. On the right is the tree of knowledge, with the
serpent coiled round its trunk; farther off a fountain of carved stonework and a stag; in the distance some high rocks.

This is probably the work of an artist of Cologne or of the Lower
Rhenish School.

FRANÇOIS CLOUET (JANET), c. 1510–1574.

11   1. CHARLOTTE DE FRANCE.

Panel.   7 × 5½ in.

Half-length portrait of a child to the waist, the face, seen in three-quarters, turned to the left. She wears a full-sleeved white frock cut square at the neck; her light hair is gathered into a white cap falling behind, secured by a gold cordon. In her hands is a gold rattle with bells, and an ivory mouthpiece. Above her head, in gold letters on the dark background: *Charlotte de France.* In the collection of drawings by Janet at Castle Howard there is one of the same child, with the inscription: *La Reyne Madellaine d'Escoce.**

Lord Ronald Gower, *Castle Howard Janets*, No. 12.
Collections—Sir Luke Schaub.
  Horace Walpole.   Sold May 17, 1842, No. 49, £58, 16s., to Mr.
    Webb.
  Mr. C. Baring Wall.
Exhibited—British Institution, 1843, No. 90.
  Royal Academy, 1879, No. 200.
Photographed, *Northbrook Gallery.*

12   2. MARECHAL DE LA MARCHE.

Panel.   6⅞ × 5⅞ in.

Half-length portrait of a man, nearly full face, turned to the left, in a black surcoat over a white dress, with full slashed sleeves. His black cap is set slanting-wise on his head, with a white drooping feather. A small medal is suspended by a gold cord round his neck. He has yellowish-red hair, moustachios, a slightly forked reddish beard, and blue eyes. Green background. In the collection of drawings by Janet at Castle Howard there is one of the same man, with the inscription: *Mons' le Marechal de la Marche.*

Lord Ronald Gower, *Castle Howard Janets*, No. 84.
Bought from Mr. Rutter, 1849.
Exhibited—Royal Academy, 1879, No. 208.
Photographed, *Northbrook Gallery.*

---

* Magdalen, 5th child of Francis I., married in 1537 James V. of Scotland, and died at Midsummer in the same year. It is said that black was first used as mourning in Scotland at her death. Burton, *History of Scotland*, iii. 166.

LUCAS CRANACH THE ELDER, 1472–1553.

13   1. CHRIST BLESSING LITTLE CHILDREN.

Panel, oak.   27¼ × 47¼ in.

Our Lord is represented standing in the middle of a crowd of mothers who have brought their children to receive his blessing. He is laying his right hand on an infant that lies on a linen cloth in its mother's arms, and grasps with its tiny hands the thumb and little finger of the Saviour's hand, as if to keep it fast.   Another child, held up by its mother, standing on our Lord's left, is caressing his chin, two more are eagerly grasping his right arm.   In the foreground, on the right, another woman is giving the breast to her babe. On the extreme left are six Apostles.   Figures three-quarter length.

Background dark ; at the top, in white capitals : LASSET DIE KINDLEIN ZV MIR KOMMEN VND WERFT INEN NICHT DEN SOLCHER IST DAS REICH GOTTES.   MARCI AM X.

Cranach painted this subject three times for the Elector of Saxony : in 1539, 1543, and 1550, as is proved by the following extracts from the Chamberlain's accounts :—

1539. "xi gulden xix gr. vor eine taffeln, das Evangelien als man die kinder zum Herren bringet."

1543. "xvij fl. iij. gr. ann xv. gulden groschen vor ein tuch daruff das Evangelium gemalet da man die kinderlein zu Christo treget."

1550. "das man die kinlein zum Heren pringt."

Paintings of this subject by Cranach are preserved in the Church of St. Wenceslaus at Naumburg, in that of St. Anne at Augsburg, and in the collection of M. Holzhausen at Frankfort.   A full-length composition of the same subject, with a castle in the background, being a pen-and-ink drawing, is in the possession of Councillor Dorrien at Leipzig.

Collection—M. E. Joly de Bammeville.
Bought June 12, 1854, £158, 11s.
C. Schuchardt, *Lucas Cranach*, Leipzig, 1851, pp. 122, 161, and 208.
Waagen, *Galleries*, p. 97.
Kugler, *Handbook*, ii. 172.
Photographed, *Northbrook Gallery.*

(11)

14   2. FREDERICK III.

Panel, oak. 8¼ × 5½ in.

Surnamed the Wise, Elector and Duke of Saxony. Bust three-quarter face, turned to the right, grey curly hair, mustachios, bushy whiskers and beard. He wears an embroidered linen shirt, a narrow black riband, a black furred robe, and a large black cap. Light-green background, with the date 1532 on the left, and Cranach's emblem beneath it. In the upper right corner, printed in black type on a piece of paper pasted on to the panel:

> "Friderich der Drit / Chur-
> furſt vnd Hertzog zu
> Sachſſen."

The lower portion of the panel is occupied by a similarly printed inscription on paper:

> "Fridrich bin ich billich genand
> Schönen frid ich erhielt im land
> Durch gros vernunfft / gedult vnd glück
> Widder manchen ertzbosen tück
> Das land ich ficret mit gebew
> Vnd Stifft ein hohe Schul auffs new
> Zu Wittemberg im Sachſſen land
> Inn der welt die ward bekand.
> Denn aus der ſelb kam Gottes wort
> Vnd thet gros ding an manchem ort
> Das Bepſtlich Reich störtzt es nidder
> Vnd bracht rechten glauben widder.
> Zum Keiſar ward erkorn ich
> Des mein alter beschweret ſich
> Da für ich Keiſar Carl erwelt
> Von dem mich nicht wand gonſt noch gelt."

Of the printed armorial achievement of the Elector pasted on to the back of the panel only a fragment remains.

Collection—M. E. Joly de Bammeville.
Bought June 12, 1854, No. 24, £13, 13s. 6d.
Waagen, *Galleries*, 97.
Exhibited—Royal Academy, 1870, No. 196.

(12)

15

3. JOHN I.

Panel, oak. $8\frac{1}{4} \times 5\frac{1}{2}$ in.

Elector and Duke of Saxony. Bust, three-quarter face, turned to the left; brown, curly hair, moustachios, bushy whiskers and beard. In similar dress to the preceding. Light-green background. In the upper left corner, in black type, on a piece of paper pasted on to the panel:

"Johans der Erft / Churfurft
vnd Hertzog zu Sachffen."

And beneath the portrait, in two columns:

" Nach meines lieben brulers end
Bleib auff mir das gantz Regimend
Mit groffer forg vnd mancher fahr
Da der Bawr toll vnd toricht war.
Die auffrhur faft inn allem land
Wie gros fewer im wald entbrand
Welches ich halff dempffen mit Gott
Der Deudfches land erret aus not
Der Rottengeifter feind ich war
Hielt im land das wort rein vnd klar
Gros drawen bittern hafs vnd neid
Umb Gottes worts willen ich leid.
Frey bekand ichs aus hertzem grund
Vnd perfonlich felbst ich da ftund.
Vor dem Keifar vnd gantzen Reich
Von Furften gfchach vor nie des gleich
Solchs gab mir mein Gott befunder
Vnd vor der wellt was ein wunder.
Vmb land vnd leut zu bringen mich
Hofft beid freund vnd feind gewislich
Ferdnand zu Romifchen Konig gmacht
Vnd fein wahl ich allein anfacht
Auff das das alte Recht beftund
Inn der gulden Bullen gegrund.
Wiewol das groffen zorn erregt
Mich doch mehr recht denn gunft bewegt
Das hertz gab Gott dem Keifar zart
Mein guter Freund zu letzt er ward.
Das ich mein end im frid befchlos
Vast fehr den Teuffel das verdros.

(13)

Erfarn hab ichs vnd zeugen thar
Wie vns die Schrifft fagt vnd ift war.
Wer Gott mitt ernft vertrawen kan
Der bleibt ein vnuerdorben man
Eszürne Teuffel odder welt
Den fieger doch zu letzt behelt."

These pictures, painted rapidly with a sure and free hand, though executed in Cranach's workshop, and under his superintendence, are most probably not his own work. In 1532 he supplied the Elector with no less than sixty pairs of these panels, as is proved by the Chamberlain's accounts of that year, in which the following item occurs: " i° ix gulden xiiijgo Lucas malhern Inhalt seiner quitantz ix par teffelein daruff gemalt sein die bede churfursten selige und lobliche gedechtnus, sonnabents nach Jubilate Inclus. iiige vor ein schrein dartzu."

Large fine portraits of these two Electors are preserved in the Grand Ducal Gallery at Weimar, in the collection of Hauptmann von Malchus at Stuttgart, and in that of Prince Basilewsky at Paris. Many copies of the smaller size are scattered about in public and private collections.

Collection—M. E. Joly de Bammeville.
Bought June 12, 1854, No. 25, £11, 11s.
Waagen, *Galleries*, 97.
Exhibited—Royal Academy, 1879, No. 200.

PETRUS CRISTUS, c. 1415–c. 1473.

1. PORTRAIT.

16

Panel, oak. 14¼ × 10¼ in.

A young man, half length, looking to the left. He is represented bareheaded, with black hair cut straight across his forehead, standing in a vaulted chamber or porch, between a doorway and a round-headed unglazed window. He wears a deep scarlet tunic with a furred collar extending half-way down the front opening. The folds of the tunic are gathered in at the waist by a girdle, which, however, is not seen; the sleeves are long, full on the shoulders, tightening towards the wrists, and ending with fur cuffs. The somewhat dark flesh tones of the throat are relieved by the narrow white collar of a linen shirt, and above the fur at the back is seen part of an under-dress in two shades of black, the flowered pattern being darker than the ground. The man's hat hangs just below his right elbow; its long, broad scarf is brought over his shoulder, and hanging down in front, partly covers a purse with a steel handle and mountings suspended from his girdle. He holds with both hands an open book of hours with red and blue initials, the binding sheathed in a cover of dark olive-green cloth, bordered by a lighter green cordon with knops and tassels at the corners. The book has a silver clasp with the letters m a r on its inner side, and a silver register with coloured ribands. On the second finger of his right hand he wears a massive gold ring; the fourth and little fingers are between the folds of a scarlet cap under the book.

The open window on the right shows a wooded landscape with cottage roofs and a winding road leading to a distant castle, towards which a man in red on a white horse is going.

The archivolt of the doorway on the left is occupied by statuettes on brackets beneath three-faced canopies; in the upper tier are a prophet holding a scroll and an apostle; in the lower, a figure with a long scroll; the bracket beneath the apostle is vacant. Beyond is seen a wall adorned with mosaic-work, and supporting a brass lion holding a shield.

On the wall of the chamber, to the left of the man and just above his head, is hung a board, to which is attached by nails an illuminated

(15)

sheet of vellum, the edge of which is protected by a narrow red riband. This has given way at the lower left corner, and the vellum has curled up from the board—a touch of truth which may serve as a sample of the faithful rendering by this master of what he had before him. The miniature represents the Vernacle, our Lord's head with its cruciform nimbus of rays and the letters א ꞷ being on a greenish-blue ground bordered by a gold band; the spaces on either side are occupied by floriated work in red, blue, green, and gold. Beneath, in two columns, is the following rhymed prayer, written, with the usual abbreviations, in red and black:

Incipit oratio ad sanctam Veronicam.

Salve, sancta facies
Nostri redemptoris,
In qua nitet species
Divini splendoris.

¶ Impressa panniculo
Nivei candoris,
Dataque Veronicæ
Signum ob amoris.

✠ Salve, nostra gloria
In hac vita dura,
Labili ac fragili
Cito transitura.

¶ Nos perduc ad patriam
O felix figura
Ad videndam faciem
Quæ est Christi pura.

Salve, o sudarium,
Nobile jocale,
Es nostrum solacium
Et memoriale.

¶ Non depicta manibus
Sculpta vel polita,
Hoc scit summus artifex
Qui te fecit ita.

¶ Esto nobis, quæsumus,
Tutum adjuvamen,
Dulce refrigerium,
Atque consolamen.

¶ Ut nobis non noceat
Hostile gravamen,
Sed fruamur requie,
Dicamus omnes amen.

Explicit.

The preciseness and microscopic neatness of hand exhibited in this picture are most remarkable.

The version of the prayer in this picture differs from any in Mone, "Lateinische Hymnen des Mittelalters," Freiburg im Breisgau, 1853, vol. i. pp. 155–157, or in Daniel, "Thesaurus Hymnologicus," Lipsiae. 1855, vol. i. p. 341, vol. ii. p. 232.*

The portrait was said to be a portrait of Philip, Duke of Burgundy, d. 1467, and ascribed to Roger de la Pasture of Tournay, better known as Van der Weyden.

Bought from Mr. Farrer, 1863.
Exhibited—Royal Academy, 1879, No. 194.
Photographed, Northbrook Gallery.

---

* See Karl Pearson, *Ein Beitrag zur Geschichte des Christusbildes im Mittelalter.* Strassburg, 1887, p. 21.

ALBRECHT DÜRER, 1471–1528.

17   1. DON MANUEL DE MENENS.

Panel, cedar.   18½ × 14½ in.

Third length of a man of about forty years of age, the face, seen
in three-quarters, turned to the right.   He has a smooth face, and
long, curly light-brown hair, and wears a black dress with broad
brown fur collar, showing the front of a fine linen shirt ; on his head,
a broad-brimmed black hat, set slanting-wise, the right side lowest.
His right hand and left arm rest on the parapet before him.   With
his left hand, on the fourth finger of which he wears a ring, he holds
a roll of paper.   Greenish-grey ground.   On the left are the remains
of an inscription :

> "D'ABABTO DV
> DON MANVELE MENENS. de
> la moutaña en los otrodes de flan."

The original of this portrait, painted by Albert Dürer in 1521,
is in the gallery at Madrid, No. 992.   See J. D. Passavant, " Die
Christliche Kunst in Spanien," Leipzig, 1853, p. 142.   This copy
has been ascribed to Quentin Matsys.

Collection—Mr. Ralph Bernal.   Sold, March 15, 1855, No. 1110, to Mr. Webb
£52, 10s.
Bought of Mr. Webb, 1855.

18   2. SQUIRRELS.

Vellum.   10 × 9⅞ in.

Two squirrels, the one in front, seen sideways, is eating an acorn ;
the other, sitting with its back to the spectator, is resting.   A water-
colour drawing, finished with great care.   Above is the date 1512,
and the cypher 𝔄.

Collection—M. E. Joly de Bammeville.
Bought, June 12, 1854, No. 4, £14, 14s.
Photographed, Northbrook Gallery.

JAN GOSSAERT OF MAUBEUGE (MABUSE),
c. 1470–1532.

19   1. VIRGIN AND CHILD ENTHRONED.

Panel, oak. 17¼ × 15½ in.

The Virgin, seated on a scarlet cushion, faces the spectator; she wears a blue dress, the drapery of which covers her feet. A tight under-sleeve of crimson is seen at the wrist of her right hand. Her long brown hair, partly covered by a white veil, falls over her shoulders. The Child, whom she supports with both arms on a linen cloth, is clutching her veil with his hands and raising himself to embrace her. The foot-pace of the throne rests on four brackets, the intervening spaces being occupied by two panels of bronze in low relief representing David and Gideon, and by a pot of blue and white stoneware containing white roses. At either end is seated an angel with his back to the base of a lofty pillar, of which only half of the lower portion is seen. The throne itself is of marble, with a conch-shaped canopy supported by a panelled semicircular back, with pilasters having bronze capitals and bases. The columns in front are adorned with angels and owls in bronze, while from rams' heads of the same material in the centre of the tympana hang festoons fastened together over the centre of the arch. Behind the throne is a hemi-cycle, between the pillars of which are seen glimpses of landscape with trees and a blue sky, contrasting well with the grey tints of the architecture and the dark drapery of the Virgin.

The composition of this picture is pleasing; the architectural details are admirably rendered, and the flesh tones are good.

This is a replica, with slight variations, of a panel (19 × 16 in.) painted by Gossaert for the convent of the Augustinian Friars at Louvain, which in 1588 was valued at £400. It was in the month of December of that year presented by the magistrates of Louvain to Philip II. of Spain, and has ever since been preserved in the Escurial.

Collection—Mr. Thomas Baring.
Exhibited—Royal Academy, 1871, No. 226.
Waagen, *Galleries*, 98.

MABUSE.

20   2. VIRGIN AND CHILD ENTHRONED,
               WITH ANGELS.

Panel, oak.   13½ × 9¾ in.

The Virgin is seated facing the spectator, in a blue dress and
mantle, falling in ample folds on the seat and foot-pace of the throne.
Her long golden hair, bound by a richly-jewelled tiara, and partly
covered by a linen kerchief, falls over her shoulders.   With her left
hand she supports the Child, who, seated on a linen cloth, looks down
at a winged cherub in red, who stands on the foot-pace of the throne,
offering him some flowers.   In front of the cherub is another playing
on the clarionet.   Opposite are four others, playing and singing from
a book.

The figures are similar to those in the Palermo triptych,* with
slight differences.   In the Palermo picture, the canopy over the throne
is supported by four highly-ornamented groups of columns, united by
depressed arches opening on to a landscape with a variety of buildings, but here the arch at the back of the throne is filled up with
solid stonework, richly carved, and there are two arches at each
side, instead of one, as here.   The fourteen statuettes which here
adorn the pillars, and the censing angels on brackets on each side
of the throne, are wanting in the triptych, where two other figures
are introduced.

In front of the base of the throne are plants in bloom: a lily, dande-
lions, marigolds, columbines, an iris, &c.   Through the arch on the
left there is an ox near the wall of an enclosed garden, in which an
angel kneels before the Virgin in the doorway of a house.   Between
the pillars on the right is a garden, in which Joseph is walking, with
a staff in his left hand and a lighted candle in his right; farther off
there is an angel on some steps leading down to water, and a swan.
Beyond are buildings and a bit of distant landscape.

The architectural accessories are all painted in grey, as also the
statues and the censing cherubs.   The draperies are bright in colour,
and the cherubs' wings are of varied plumage.

Collection—Sir Thomas Baring.
Waagen. *Art and Artists*, iii. 43.
    „   *Galleries*, 98.
Exhibited—Royal Academy, 1872, No. 229.
Photographed, *Northbrook Gallery*.

---
* There is a coloured drawing of the Palermo triptych in the possession of the Arundel
Society.

21   3. PHILIP LE BEL.

Panel, oak: the picture and frame of one piece. Height, 9¾–12½ in.;
breadth, 6¼–8¾ in.

Half-length portrait of a young man, three-quarters face, turned
to the left. His crimson dress, faced with fur, open in front, shows
the collar of the Golden Fleece, which he wears over a tight-sleeved
blue under-dress stitched with gold, and an embroidered cambric
shirt. On his head a greenish-blue cap. His right hand and left
arm rest on the chamfer of the frame; in his left hand he holds a
roll of paper.

Pasted on the back is a piece of parchment with handwriting
apparently of the latter half of the sixteenth century:

> Cestui pourtraict est de
> phillippe daufuriche fils
> de Larchiduc Maximilien
> et dame Marie ducesse
> de bourgoigne; ce prinche
> prinst pour femme Jeanne
> fille du Roy ferrand: il
> mourust en Espaigne
> en 1505 et gist a granaele.

Collection—M. E. Joly de Bammeville.
Bought June 12, 1854, No. 22, £13, 2s. 6d.
Exhibited—Royal Academy, 1879, No. 197.

HANS HOLBEIN, 1497–1543.

22   JOHN HERBSTER.

Paper, pasted on to a panel of deal. 16 × 10¾ in.

The bust of an original-looking middle-aged man, the face seen in three-quarters, turned to the right, with a brown beard and long hair. He wears a dark-grey dress and a large, bright-red cap. The background is an open archway of Renaissance architecture, showing the blue sky behind. From the centre of the arch hang two festoons of fruit and foliage, the ends of which are held by two winged boys seated on the capitals of the pillars. Above the heads of these boys are two little tablets supported by festoons, the one on the left containing the date, " 1.5.16," the other the age of Herbster, " ÆT. 57," now almost effaced. On a sort of parapet or plinth below is the inscription:

     IOANNES HERBSTER PICTOR OPORINI PATER.

This masterly portrait is most carefully executed, in those yellowish flesh-tones of which Holbein was so fond. It bears considerable affinity to the altar-piece of St. Sebastian, executed in 1512, now in the Museum of Augsburg, but is of more delicate rendering. The architecture, of a golden tone, is pleasing.

But little is known of the artist here represented. His name is inscribed in the registers of the guild of the painters of Basel, " Zunft zum Himmel," but his works are unknown. Füssli tells us that he was in the battle of Pavia in 1512. He was father of the famous printer of Basel, Oporinus, and we may perhaps safely deduce from the date of this portrait that Holbein removed from Augsburg to Basel at latest in 1516.*

Engraved as a Van Eyck by Garreau (reversed) in Le Brun, "Galerie des Peintres Flamands, Hollandais et Allemands," Paris, 1792, tom. i. pl. 2. In this plate one of the tablets bears the cypher H.H.

Collection—Mr. J. Bayntun. Sold April 8, 1853, No. 251, to Mr. Farrer, £81. Bought from Mr. Farrer, 1854.
Waagen, *Galleries*, 97.
R. N. Wornum, *Hans Holbein*, London, 1867, pp. 104 and 105.
Kugler, *Handbook*, i. 201.
Exhibited—Royal Academy, 1879, No. 191.
Photographed, *Northbrook Gallery*.

* Dr. Ernst Stükelberg of Basle, a descendant of Herbster, was kind enough to send me a copy of a portrait of him as a young man which is in his possession.

(21)

QUENTIN MATSYS, 1450–1529.

23 VIRGIN AND CHILD ENTHRONED.

Panel, oak. 29¼ × 24¼ in.

The Virgin is seated on a throne with a conch-shaped canopy, having a cloth of honour of gold brocade, diapered with flowers and birds, and curtains which are drawn back on either side. She wears a dark-blue dress cut square at the neck, showing a good deal of fine linen, full lilac sleeves, and a red mantle which has fallen back from her shoulders. With her left arm she sustains the Child, seated on a crimson cushion on the arm of the throne, and in her right holds two cherries. Her face, seen in three-quarters, is turned to the right. Her hair, confined by a double row of pearls with a jewel in front, is partly hidden by a very thin gauze veil. The Child has both arms round his mother's neck, and is kissing her.

Through a round-arched opening on the left is seen a hilly landscape, with water a castle and trees, shut in by distant mountains.

On a parapet in the front are an apple and a bunch of grapes.

This picture, formerly ascribed to Leonardo da Vinci, is an early copy of a very fine work of Quentin Matsys, now in the Museum at Amsterdam, but, in the middle of the seventeenth century, in the possession of Peter Stevens, almoner and churchwarden of the Cathedral of Antwerp, where it was seen by Alexander Van Fornenbergh, who gives a long description of it in his work "Den Antwerpschen Protheus ofte Cyclopschen Apelles," Antwerp, 1658. Another early copy is in the Berlin Museum, No. 561.

Engraved by C. F.L. Taurel in "L'Art Chrétien en Hollande et en Flandre," Amsterdam, 1872–60. 6¼ × 5¼ in.

Bought from Mr. Martin Colnaghi, 1864, as by Van Orley.

MARTIN SCHAFFNER, 16th Century.

24   MARRIAGE OF THE VIRGIN.

Panel. 13½ × 11¼ in.

The ceremony is represented as taking place in a three-aisled
temple.   The high-priest wears a cloth-of-gold tunic and cope, and
a mitre adorned with pearls ; over all is a scarlet stole, one end of
which is wrapped round the hands of the Virgin and Joseph.   Behind, on the right, is an attendant with a pastoral staff, and on
the left, another in a scarlet cap.   On the left are three figures, and
on the right a fourth, assisting at the ceremony.

Collection—Rev. James Heath.
Bought by the Earl of Northbrook, April 10, 1880, No. 164, £34, 13s.

JAN VAN EYCK, c. 1390–1440.

25   VIRGIN AND CHILD.

Panel, oak. 10¾ × 7½ in.

The Virgin, three-quarters length, is seated under a canopy with a cloth of honour of olive-green diapered with flowers, bordered with a narrow scarlet riband.

She wears a dark-blue rather low dress and a crimson mantle; both have richly-jewelled orphreys. Her long hair, which falls in undulating masses over her shoulders, is confined by a band fastened above the forehead by a jewel composed of a ruby surrounded with pearls. She supports with her right hand the Infant Saviour, seated on a linen cloth on her lap. He is taking from his mother a nosegay of red and white pinks, and with his right hand caresses a paroquet.

This is a genuine picture, well modelled and painted with great finish. It closely resembles the central figure in the altar-piece painted for Canon George de Pale, formerly in the Collegiate Church of S. Donatian at Bruges, and now in the Museum of the Academy of that city, terminated in 1436. This little panel is attributed to the year 1437.

The back of the panel is painted stone-colour.

Collection—M. E. Joly de Bammeville. Sold June 12, 1854, No. 29, £64, 1s., to Mr. Nieuwenhuys.
Bought from Mr. Nieuwenhuys, 1857.
Weale, *Catalogue du Musée de l'Académie de Bruges*, Bruges, 1864, pp. 12–17.
   ,,   *Bruges et ses Environs*, 4ᵉ édition, Bruges, 1882, p. 54.
   ,,   *Revue de l'Art Chrétien*, 3ᵉ Série, Lille, 1883, tom. i. p. 66.
Exhibited—Royal Academy, 1872, No. 234.

JAN VAN HEMESSEN, 14..-156..

26   CALL OF ST. MATTHEW.

Panel, oak.   27 × 33½ in.

On the left, our Lord, in grey, facing the spectator, is turning to the right, and addressing Matthew, who is bending forward across the counter of his office, holding in his left hand a singularly-shaped hat, round which is wound a brown scarf. On the counter are a coffer, a dish containing coin, a money-box, an inkstand and pen, and some account-books, one of which is open, showing the entries: " Item, vertolt in Juli . . . Item, noch vertolt den xxj Augusti . . . Item, vertolt in den iiij in Sept. . . . Item, vertolt in den x. Octob."

On the left, outside the office, are St. Peter in green, and two other apostles, and in the background two towers with a mountain in the distance.

On the right are several files of papers, and in the middle a tablet, suspended by a ring, bearing: " Mat. 9a . . . Mar. 2b. . . . Luc. 5f."

Painted with a delicate touch, in a warm, transparent tone.

Formerly attributed to Quentin Matsys. A somewhat similar picture, signed Jan Van Hemmessen, is in the Museum at Antwerp.

Collection—Mr. Edward Puckle of Flushing, near Falmouth, 1845-50.
Bought from Mr. F. K. Fowell, 1850.
Exhibited—Royal Academy, 1872, No. 239.
Photographed, *Northbrook Gallery.*

BERNARD VAN ORLEY, c. 1489–1542.

27   CHARLES V.

Panel. Height, 14⅜ × 11½ in.

The Emperor is represented on a white charger, advancing towards the left, holding an arrow in his right hand, and the reins of his horse in his left, which rests on the pommel of his sword. In front of him on the ground lies a Moorish king, clutching at a sceptre with his left hand, and at the same time raising his right as if to implore the conqueror's mercy. The Emperor wears a rich suit of armour, sleeves of blue and red shot silk, a fantastically-shaped helmet with a bunch of drooping plumes, and long, untanned leather boots with spurs. His horse's reins are formed of crimson scarves knotted together. The Moorish king has a dark-blue furred robe with gold clasp, and green and red shot silk sleeves; he wears his crown outside a greenish-yellow conical hat with turned-up border lined with white. He has a beard, moustachio, and long hair.

This group is, as it were, framed by an archway of Renaissance style a little behind the figures, the view of all but the slightly clouded sky being shut out by a ruined stone wall, on which a shrub has taken root.

Formerly attributed to Albert Dürer.

Collections—Sold at Christie's, Jan. 13, 1816, No. 51, £4, 6s., to Mr. Hibler.
            Mr. Pilgrim. Put up March 5, 1824, No. 60, bought in at £8.
            Sold April 29, 1825, No. 33, £5, 5s., to Mr. Crawford.
            Mr. Samuel Rogers.
Bought, May 2, 1856, No. 555, £100.
Waagen, *Treasures*, ii. 270.
Photographed, *Northbrook Gallery*.

DUTCH AND FLEMISH SCHOOLS.

JAN ASSELYN, 1610–1660.

28 ITALIAN LANDSCAPE.

Canvas. 21¼ × 25¾ in.

In the centre, a young woman in blue on a donkey holds up a
bird, for which a dog is jumping, to the amusement of a youth who
kneels at her right and is pulling up his stockings. To the right are
three cows, a goat, and some sheep watering in a pool of clear water
at the foot of some ruins. On the left is a road with goats and a
goatherd in the distance. Blue sky with a few light clouds. Signed
to the right.

This picture is one of the best works of the master, painted in his
later manner, after his return to Holland, between 1651 and 1660 ;
the figures treated in the manner of Peter Van Laer.

Collections—Prince Galitzin, Paris, February 28, 1825.
    Verstolk.
Bought in 1846.
Smith, v. 276.
Waagen, *Treasures*, ii. 186. "In harmonious coolness, firmly-treated chiaroscuro,
and truth of detail, this picture rivals Du Jardin."
Kugler, *Handbook*, ii. 446.

LUDOLPH BACKHUISEN, 1631–1708.

29   1. VIEW ON THE BRILL.

Canvas. 16½ × 23½ in.

A view on the Brill river during a stiff breeze, with heavy clouds. On the right is a bank with two slender trees growing on it, at the foot of which are two men. A little way off, on the extreme right, is a cottage. A small boat with three men in it is putting off from the shore, on which the waves are breaking. On the left is a lugger under brown main and white foresails, and beyond her are several fishing-boats. The tower of the Brill Church is seen in the distance on the left. Signed *L.B.*, on the bank, on the right.

Collection—Duc de Berri.
Exhibited at Christie's for sale in 1834, price £320.
Bought from Mr. Nieuwenhuys, 1849.
Smith, vi. 449, No. 146. "Few pictures by the master possess more taste and true feeling for Nature."
Waagen, *Treasures*, ii. 188. "A picture of the finest quality."
Photographed, *Northbrook Gallery.*

30   2. A BREEZE AT SEA.

Canvas. 30⅞ × 49½ in.

In the front, on the left, is a buoy, and beyond a yacht with a number of people of quality on board; at the stern a shield *or*, a lion rampant *gules*, surmounted by a crown; below the shield, the motto: CONCORDIA RES PARVÆ CRESCONT; beyond, a frigate. On the right, a boat with three men, one engaged with a sail, two others dragging in a net; beyond, a frigate anchoring, and in the distance other vessels. Blue sky with dark masses of clouds to the left. Signed, on the boat, on the right: *L. Back.*

Collections—Mr. George Hibbert.
        Sir Thomas Baring.
Bought, June 3, 1848, No. 130, £283, 10s.
Waagen, *Treasures*, ii. 188. "Of rich and happy composition, and carefully executed in cool, clear tones. It belongs to the best period of the master."
Kugler, *Handbook*, ii. 469.

NICHOLAS BERCHEM, 1624-1683.

31   MUSICAL PEASANTS PASSING A FORD.

Panel.   11½ × 17½ in.

On the left a man and a woman on horseback, singing and playing, are crossing a ford, followed by two peasants on foot and a dog. In the centre a man is riding down to the ford driving some cattle before him, while another drives two sheep up the bank. On the other side of the ford there is a wood, a castle, and distant hills; some feathery trees to the right. Warm evening light. Signed to the left : *Berchem.*

Collection—Duc de Berri.
Imported by Mr. Hume, 1840.
Bought through Mr. Chaplin, 1849.
Smith, ix. 616, No. 29.
Waagen, *Treasures,* ii. 186.

GERRIT BERCK HEYDE, 1638–1698.

32   1. MARKET-PLACE, HAARLEM.

Panel.   23¼ × 32¼ in.

View on the Great Market-place. Facing the spectator is the Town-house, a red brick building with an octagonal tower, erected 1630–1633. On either side are several gabled houses. The square is enlivened by numerous figures of men; from a narrow street (the Groote Hout Straat) on the left, a lady in blue skirt and yellow jacket is advancing towards the middle.

On one gable of the Town-house is a shield bearing *gules*, a sword erect *argent*, the hilt and pommel *or*, with the motto: VICIT VIM VIRTVS ANNO 1633, and below it a statue of Justice. Over a door to the right: S.P.Q.H. ANNO 1630. On the roof a stork and two nests. Blue sky with a few light clouds. Signed and dated on a beam of a house on the left: GERRIT BERK HEYDE F. 1661.

The figures are by his elder brother, Job Berck-Heyde (1630–1693).

Collections—Château de Loenen, near Loenen.
        Verstolk.
Bought in 1846.
Smith, v. 410.
Waagen, *Treasures*, ii. 188. "The masterly treatment, the striking sunny effect, and unusually careful execution, render this picture very attractive."
Kugler, *Handbook*, ii. 509.
Photographed, *Northbrook Gallery*.

33 2. MARKET-PLACE, HAARLEM.

Panel. 23½ × 32½ in.

View of the Great Market-place, taken from near the Town-house, showing the great Church with the curious stalls underneath it. There are several gabled houses near the foreground to the right, as well as farther off to the left. Many groups of figures are scattered about the square, among them a gentleman on horseback with a couple of greyhounds. This picture was probably painted to match the preceding one. Signed G. Berck Heyde, 1669.

Collection—Colonel A. Ridgway. Sold January 15, 1886, £290, 5s.
Bought by the Earl of Northbrook from Messrs. Colnaghi, 1886.

FERDINAND BOL, 1611–1681.

34 1. THE PEARL NECKLACE.

56½ × 70 in.

In the centre a young lady stands, facing the spectator, looking at herself in a mirror placed on a table covered with a red and yellow carpet, as she fastens a necklace of pearls to her left shoulder. She wears a yellow silk dress with a skirt of white satin. On her right is seated a gentleman with a silver-topped cane in his right hand. He is looking at her reflection in the glass. On the table, to the right, are a casket of jewels, a book, and a vase. The figures, three-quarter length, are life-size. Signed on the back of the mirror : *F. Bol fecit* 1649.

Collection—A Collection in Amsterdam.
    Verstolk.

Bought in 1846.

Waagen, *Treasures*, ii. 182. "In power and transparency of general effect, in the delicate golden tones of the female figure, and in the truthful reddish colouring and careful execution of the man, this picture may be considered as one of the *chefs d'œuvre* of this scholar of Rembrandt."

Kugler, *Handbook*, ii. 377.

Burger, 251. "Il n'y a rien à dire contre cette belle peinture, si ce n'est qu'elle imite par trop un des célèbres Rembrandt de Buckingham palace, la femme du Bourgmestre Pancras, laquelle est en train d'admirer devant une glace les boucles d'oreilles que lui a sans doute données son mari, assis près d'elle."

35   2. SCENE FROM GUARINI'S "PASTOR
FIDO."

Canvas. 54 × 75 in.

A composition of nine figures. In the centre, a lady in white
satin, with a blue mantle over her left shoulder and arm, is crowning
with flowers a woman in yellow, who holds a bow in her left hand.
On the right are four other women, the foremost in crimson holding
a crook, and two dogs. On the left is another woman in a rustic
hat, and in the mid-distance two more seated. Signed.

Collections—Sir Charles Bagot. Sold June 18, 1836, No. 40, £121, 16s., to
        Mr. Brondgeest.
       Verstolk.
Bought in 1846.
Smith, vii. 245. "One of his finest productions."
Waagen, Treasures, ii. 183.
Kugler, Handbook, ii. 376. "An admirable picture of his later time."

36   3. ADMIRAL DE RUYTER.

Canvas. 42½ × 34 in.

The Admiral, a full-length figure, life-size, is represented standing,
facing the spectator; he is in full dress, cloth-of-gold uniform, with
black robe over it, and wears the collar of the Order of Saint Michael.
He has long black hair, a black moustachio, and a grey imperial. In
his right hand he holds his staff of office, while his left rests on his
hip. On the right is a red curtain, looped up; on the left, in the
background, a ship of war with the Dutch colours.

Bol painted the portrait of the Admiral nine times; for Louis XIV.,
William III., the Admiralty Houses of Amsterdam, Hoorn, Enkhuisen, and Medemblik, and for the town of Flushing, his birthplace;
this last is now in the National Museum. Van der Helst painted
him thrice; two of his portraits were in 1847 in the possession of
Mr. Elias, burgomaster of Amsterdam.

Collections—Admiralty House, Enkhuisen.
        M. J. Vaillant, Director of Town Wharves, Amsterdam. Sold to
           Mr. Brondgeest.
       Verstolk.
Bought in 1846.

JAN BOTH, c. 1610–c. 1650.

37   1. THE FAREWELL.

Canvas.   42 × 39 in.

In the foreground, on the right, two gentlemen on horseback are
bidding each other farewell, hat in hand, while a guide, carrying a
gun, is slowly moving off to the left.   On the road to the right are
two horsemen going up to a wooden bridge over a stream in the mid-
distance, towards which two laden mules, followed by a man and
woman, are coming down from the left.   Under the bridge is a
waterfall, which is seen again falling from the high rocks which
form the background on the right.   Blue evening sky, with brownish
clouds.   Signed on the left.   The figures are by the artist's brother
Andreas.

Indifferent etching by C. Josi, 10½ × 8¾ in.
Collections—Mr. John Van Hollenhoven.   Sold, April 2, 1794, No. 11, for 506
florins, to Mr. Yver.
Mr. C. Josi.   Put up at Christie's, March 23, 1822, No. 64 ; bought
in at £581, 15s.   Again put up at Christie's, May 16, 1829,
No. 84 ; bought in at £372, 15s.
Mr. Nieuwenhuys.   Sold to the Hon. G. Vernon.
Hon. G. Vernon.   Sold, April 16, 1831, £297, 3s., to Mr. Woodin.
Mr. Ralph Fletcher.
Bought June 28, 1851, No. 61, £580.
Smith, vi. 190, No. 55, and ix. 733, No. 8.
Waagen, *Treasures*, ii. 187.
Exhibited—Royal Academy, 1872, No. 181.

38   2. LANDSCAPE.

Panel.   9⅞ × 12⅞ in.

In the centre, two men, three goats, and a donkey by the roadside ; another man is following a cow down the road. On the left, on higher ground, a man and a boy are walking along the foot of some high rocks overgrown with bushes. On the right a stream ; in the distance blue hills. Blue sky. Signed to the left.

Collection—Sir Thomas Baring. Sold June 3, 1848, No. 85, £48, 6s.
Bought from Mr. Smith, 1848.
Waagen, *Treasures*, ii. 187. "Charming in feeling and solidly carried out."

———

JAN BREUGEL, 1565–1642.

39   TRAVELLING PEASANTS.

Panel.   8½ × 11⅞ in.

A clump of trees stands in the centre on a rising ground, across which a road runs, with groups of figures, waggons, horses, &c., passing along it. Blue distance, with trees and towns.

Collection—Mr. George Smith.
Bought by the Earl of Northbrook, April 10, 1856, £32, 11s.

WILLEM BUITENWEG, 17th Century.

40   LANDSCAPE.

Panel. 10¼ × 13½ in.

On a road in the foreground is a white horse, and a man sitting on a felled tree with a dog at his side. On the right, a hill with sheep. In the distance, on the right, some low hills. The sky to the left is covered with heavy clouds. Signed on the right : W. BUITENWEG.

Formerly ascribed to John Wynants.

Collection—Earl of Beverley.
Bought in 1851.

CATS, 17th Century.

41   THE DOCTOR.

Canvas. 30½ × 26 in.

On the right is seated an elderly man, probably a doctor, wearing a black robe with a white collar, and a black cap. His right hand rests on the arm of his chair, his left on some papers lying on a table covered with a Turkey cloth ; one of the sheets of paper has on it a full-length drawing of a human skeleton. On the arm of the chair is inscribed the man's age : ÆT. 50. He is looking towards a woman with a white kerchief on her head, who is approaching him from the left, holding her left hand up to her face as if in grief, and leading a little girl with a basket on her arm. A similar basket lies empty on the ground before the man.

The background is divided into two by a pier supporting two

round-headed arches. That on the right, behind the man, is furnished with a curtain looped up to the left; beyond it is seen a bookcase, and through the arch on the left a window glazed with roundels, through which are seen a cottage and trees. On the sill is a jar with the words: CATS F.

This subject is enclosed in an oval frame, of which the half to the left is composed of human bones, and that to the right of leaves and flowers; hanging from the top is a round ball, and above it a scroll with the words: MEMENTO MORI, ANNO 1662.

Formerly attributed to Thomas Wyck and to Gerbrand Van den Eeckhout.

History.

1819, July 17. Catalogue of a sale at Christie's, No. 28, belonging to Mr. W. Smith; bought in at £50, 6s. 6d.

1821, July 27. Catalogue of a sale at Christie's, No. 52, belonging to Mr. W. Smith; bought in at £60.

1825, June 25. Catalogue of a sale at Christie's, No. 77, belonging to Mr. W. Smith; bought in at £34, 13s.

In the catalogues of these three sales the picture is attributed to G. Van den Eeckhout. The dimensions not being given, it is impossible to say whether it is the work described above. Having sought in vain for any notice of a painter of the name of Cats living in 1662, we think it well to give the following extracts from other sale catalogues :—

1835, July 4. Collection of William Smith, Esq., M.P. for Norwich, sold at Christie's, No. 115—Cats: Interior of an apartment, with an advocate seated at a table, and a woman with a basket; painted with a capital effect of sunshine. £31, 10s. to Parsons.

1836, January 30. Catalogue of a sale at Christie's, No. 90, belonging to R. E.—Cats :—Interior of a physician's apartment; a clever copy. £1, 10s. to Johnson.

1836, April 23. Collection of Mr. Scott, sold at Christie's, No. 29—Rembrandt: Portrait of the physician Cats seated at a table, with a woman and child about to consult him; with admirable effect of light. Bought in at £56, 3s. 6d.

Collection—Sir Thomas Baring.

Bought, June 3, 1848, No. 73, £17, 6s. 6d., as by Thomas Wyck.

GONZALES COQUES or COCX, 1618-1684.

42   GENTLEMAN AND LADY ON HORSEBACK.

Panel, oak.   16⅛ × 14⅞ in.

A gentleman, bareheaded, riding a prancing white horse to the left, with a sword at his side and a whip in his right hand, which is raised.   Behind him, a lady in a low yellow dress and a hat with feathers, on a bay horse, holding a fan in her left hand.   On the extreme right, a negro servant, standing with his master's hat in his hand, is looking at a spaniel, which is admirably painted.   Landscape with trees, a stream, and a distant church.   Blue evening sky with clouds.

This picture is painted in Coques's best manner, based on the study of Peter Breughel and of Anthony Van Dyck.   There is much character in the heads; the figures are elegant and refined; the execution of the details careful, without undue prominence being given to them.

Collections—Given by the Queen of the Netherlands to the Prince of Orange
in 1817, as a birthday present.
King of Holland.   Sold August 12, 1850, No. 61, to M. Nieuwen-
huys, 800 florins.
Bought from M. Nieuwenhuys, 1851.
Nieuwenhuys, *Review*, 95.
Description de la Collection de S. A. le Prince d'Orange à Bruxelles.
Bruxelles, 1837, 34.
Photographed, *Northbrook Gallery.*

ALBERT CUYP, 1605-1691.

43   1. A GIRL.

Panel. 35 × 32 in.

Full-length figure of a girl of about six years of age, standing holding a red rose in her hand. She is seen nearly full face, has fair hair and blue eyes, and wears a dark-green dress slashed and trimmed with yellow, a white apron, white collar and cuffs trimmed with lace, lace head-dress, red coral bracelets and gold necklace and cross. Behind her, a chair with red leather seat and back, and a dark curtain.

This picture has been lengthened a little to match another one.

Collection—Mr. Thomas Baring.

44   2. VIEW NEAR DORDRECHT.

Panel. 28½ × 35½ in.

View of the river Merewede, near Dordrecht, with several vessels. One bank only is seen, stretching nearly across to the left. In front, on the right, are several fishing and cargo vessels, with their sails up, lying near the shore; and in front of them are two boats, in one of which are two men, and in the other a boy fishing. To the left is a two-oared row-boat approaching with eleven passengers, some of whom appear to be persons of distinction. The river is skirted by bushes and trees, and enlivened by a number of other vessels, the most distant of which are barely visible through the warm golden haze of a fine summer morning.

This picture is painted with the same brilliancy as the well-known picture by the same master at Dorchester House, where it forms part of Mr. Holford's splendid collection.

Collections—Mr. Johan Goll von Frankestein, Amsterdam. Sold, July 1, 1833,
       No. 14, for 10,200 florins, to Mr. Brondgeest.
       Verstolk.
Bought in 1846.
Smith, v. 346, No. 216.
Waagen, *Treasures*, ii. 187.
Kugler, *Handbook*, ii. 462.
Burger, 267.
Viardot, 155.
Exhibited—British Institution, 1850, No. 9.
       Royal Academy, 1871, No. 209, and 1880, No. 81.

45   3. PRINCE HENRY FREDERICK AT THE SIEGE
OF BREDA.

Panel. 12¼ × 16½ in.

View near Breda during a siege. On the right, in the foreground,
is Prince Henry Frederick on a bay horse, and behind him two
mounted officers. On the left are a number of people near some
tents, and towards the centre are four men carrying a soldier on a
stretcher. In the middle distance are an officer on horseback and
others looking on at the firing, while in the background is seen the
town, with its church-tower rising high above the other buildings.
Blue sky with a few light clouds. The appearance is that of morning, the general effect fresh and airy. A careful, well-preserved
picture; the details delicately painted. Signed on the left.

Collections—Marquis of Bute. Sold, June 8, 1822, No. 64, £63, to Mr. Foules.
     Mr. Charles Baird.
Bought May 10, 1849, No. 54, £107, 2s.
Smith, v. 361, No. 265.
Waagen, *Treasures*, ii. 186.
Exhibited—British Institution, 1845, No. 19.
     Royal Academy, 1872, No. 162, and 1885. No. 73.

DAVID DE HEEM, 1570–1632.

46   FRUIT.

Panel. 20½ × 15½ in.

In a stone round-headed niche are a gilt vase supported by a bird's
foot, a salver of Venetian glass, and a tall drinking-glass, a pepper-
caster, and a gold watch with an open lid and a blue riband attached
to it, a melon, some grapes and chestnuts, and a bramble branch
with blackberries. A snail, a caterpillar, and some other insects,
are introduced about the fruit. On a shelf below are oysters, a lemon
partly peeled, a knife, &c.

Bought from Mr. Martin Colnaghi, 1861.

JAN, SON OF DAVID DE HEEM, 1600–1684.

47   FRUIT AND FLOWERS.

Panel. 14½ × 18 in.

On a table, the top of which is covered with a dark lilac cloth, is a metal dish containing purple and green grapes, a couple of peaches, one of which is cut open, a nectarine, a spray of convolvulus, two or three ears of corn, and a carnation. To the left stands a glass of light-coloured liquor.

Signed on left: J. D. De Heem, f.

Collection—Mr. W. Jones of Clytha.
Bought May 8, 1852, No. 29, £8, 8s.

PETER DE HOOCH, 1632–1681.

48   THE PET PARROT.

Canvas. 31½ × 26 in.

On the right, with his back to the fireplace, a man is sitting at a table drinking. At the end of the table, to the left, a little girl is standing on a chair, looking up at a parrot in a cage. A maid-servant, standing on the farther side of the chair, is taking care of the child and at the same time holds out a glass of wine to a lady who is dipping a cake in the wine and coaxing the head of the bird. A brown and white spaniel is jumping up, with its forepaws on the child's chair. The lady, who wears a red velvet jacket trimmed with white fur, has her back to a window on the left, from which the light streams into the room. On the table, covered with a white cloth, are bread, cheese, and fruit. On the mantelpiece are a bottle and some cups, and above it a picture of a woman reclining at full length.

Collections—Duc de Berri.
Imported by Mr. Hume, 1840.
Bought from Mr. Chaplin, 1854.
Smith, ix. 565, No. 6.
Waagen, *Galleries*, 99.

DE VLIEGER.

CLAUDE DE JONGHE, 16 . . –1663.

49   OLD LONDON BRIDGE.

Panel. 17 × 39½ in.

The view is taken from the north side, a little above the bridge. On the left, in the foreground, is a jetty alongside of which are three boats, the smallest of which is empty ; in the second is a man with a package which he is carrying to the farther end of the boat. In the largest boat, which has a cabin with blue drapery, are seven persons. A gentleman, two ladies, and a boy are walking down the jetty. On the river, above the bridge, are fourteen row-boats, whilst between the bridge and the tower are three large vessels lying off the wharves. The drawbridge is down ; two men on it are the only figures on the bridge. Blue morning sky with clouds.

Signed on building, on the left : C. DE JONGHE, 1650.

A larger replica of this picture (25 × 48 in.), formerly at the Hague (collection of Mr. Wm. Van Wouw, sold 29th May 1764, No. 100, sold for 36 florins, and collection of Mr. A. J. Carré, sold 6th June 1820, No. 40), is now in the South Kensington Museum. Another, from the Marquis of Exeter's collection, was sold in 1888.

Collections—Wynn Ellis. Sold May 27, 1876, No. 17, £525.
        Mr. John Heugh.
Bought by the Earl of Northbrook, May 11, 1878, No. 252, £787, 10s.

SIMON DE VLIEGER, 1600–1657.

50   SCHEVELINGHEN.

Canvas. 23½ × 38 in.

On the right is a village with a church with a low square tower on a headland, from which a jetty runs out in the mid-distance. About it are seven fishing-boats. The scene is enlivened by nearly forty figures, the chief group of which is collected round some fish lying on the ground near the centre. In the distance, on the left, is a ship. Blue sky with clouds.

Signed on the right.

Collection—Earl of Beverley.
Bought in 1854.

EMANUEL DE WITTE, 1607–1692.

51   1. OUDE KERK, AMSTERDAM.

Panel. 17⅞ × 13½ in.

In a pulpit against a pillar on the farther side of the nave, a minister is preaching to a congregation, some seated, others standing. In the foreground, to the right, is a dog, and another sits by the pillar in the centre. On the right is an organ with blue shutters. Signed on the wooden vaulting, with the date 1669.

Collections—M. Tjaard Anthony van Iddekinge, Amsterdam. Sold April 25,
        1838, No. 29, 550 florins, to Mr. Brondgeest.
            Verstolk.
Bought in 1846.
Waagen, *Treasures*, ii. 188.

52   2. OUDE KERK, AMSTERDAM.

Panel. 17⅞ × 13½ in.

The companion picture. In the foreground, on the left, a man in a hat and cloak with a dog, talking to a woman with a basket on her arm and a little girl by her side. In the background, four other figures, a pulpit, an organ, a chandelier, hatchments with coats of arms, and a mural monument.

Signed on the base of a pillar, on the right, with the date 1669.

Collections—M. Tjaard Anthony van Iddekinge, Amsterdam. Sold April 25,
        1838, No. 30, 500 florins, to Mr. Brondgeest.
            Verstolk.
Bought in 1846.
Waagen, *Treasures*, ii. 188.
Photographed, *Northbrook Gallery*.

GERARD DOW, 1613–1675.

THE PHILOSOPHER.

Panel. 12¼ × 9¾ in.

Interior of a room, with a round-headed window on the left, near which an old man sits in an arm-chair. He wears a lilac cap and robe, with collar and facings of fur, and is writing in a large book which he supports with his left arm. Before him is an easel with a panel on it. On his left, in the background, are two steps, with a table on the upper one, covered with a light-blue cloth, on which are a globe, a candlestick, and a book, bearing on its edges the signature G. Dov. A blue curtain suspended from the rafters is looped up behind a base viol hanging to a nail in the pillar. In the foreground, on the right, are a drum, a helmet, and a shield. Above hangs a six-branched brass chandelier.

Dow has represented the same interior and several of the accessories in other pictures, e.g., in a still smaller one belonging to Mrs. Morrison.

This picture was no doubt painted before 1640, as it shows in a marked manner the influence of Rembrandt. It should be compared with two paintings by that master now in the Louvre, which were formerly in the Choiseul Gallery, and are engraved (Nos. 44 and 45) in the illustrated catalogue of that collection.

Collections—M. Van Zwieten, The Hague. Sold April 12, 1741, No. 65, 400 florins.
M. Adrian Leonard van Heteren.
Museum of Amsterdam. Sold August 4, 1828, by the Director of the Museum, No. 74, 546 florins.
Mr. Emmerson.
Mr. Charles Brind.
Bought, May 10, 1849, No. 65, £96, 12s.
Smith, i. 36, No. 103. "This little jewel was formerly in the possession of King William III."
Waagen, *Treasures*, ii. 183.
Exhibited—British Institution, 1848, No. 151.

KAREL DU JARDIN, 1625–1678.

54   THE MANÈGE.

Canvas. 20 × 18 in.

A wooded landscape with a clear open space surrounded by trees. On the left, a cavalier is buckling on his spurs preparatory to mounting a black horse held by a page in blue; another cavalier on a chestnut horse is looking on. In the middle of the foreground are two dogs; on the right a man riding a prancing grey horse. In the background another cavalier is about to jump over a bar held by a groom between two posts. Two men in cloaks stand looking on. Blue sky with a few clouds. Signed on the right with the date 1654.

Collections—M. Montaleau. Sold 1802, 7020 francs.
     M. Emler. Sold 1809, 10,001 francs.
     M. Alexis de la Hante. Bought in, 1821, £442, 1s.
     Mr. Beckford, Fonthill Abbey. Sold 1823, £304, 10s.
     The Hon. Long Pole Wellesley, Brussels.
     M. de Morny. Sold 1848, £651.
Bought from Mr. Farrer, 1849.
Smith, v. 249, No. 48.
Waagen, *Treasures*, ii. 186. "In the delicate silver tone of the whole, the truth of the details, and the tender execution, all the most admired qualities of the master are united."
Bürger, 301–303. "De la plus belle qualité du maître."
Viardot, 155.
Exhibited—Manchester, 1857, No. 971.

CORNELIS DUSART, 16 . .–1704.

55   THE FATHER'S RETURN.

Panel.   18 × 14¼ in.

Interior of a cottage. A peasant woman is seated in a long low wicker-chair before a fire, nursing a baby in scarlet, stretching out its arms towards its father, who has apparently just come home from the fair, and holds up a punchinello. Behind the woman stands a boy. In the background is a cupboard, on the top of which are a ham on a dish, a green earthenware jug, a basket, &c. ; and above, some dried fish hanging against the wall, a white dish, a saucepan-cover, and a spoon in a rack. Farther to the left is a bed in a recess, with a sword hanging from a nail. In the foreground are a broom. a box with linen, &c., and a pair of tongs.

Signed above the boy's head : COR. DUSART, 1680.

Collections—M. Héris of Brussels.
         Verstolk.
Bought in 1856.
Waagen, *Treasures*, ii. 185.
   „   *Handbook*, ii. 301.

JAN FYT, 1609–1661.

56   1. CATS FIGHTING.

Canvas.   28½ × 54 in.

On the left a tankard and two metal rings. In the centre a dish, and on the right a large repoussé vessel with some artichokes in it. A basket of vegetables, some spoons, and a knife and a fork are falling from a shelf on the right, having been knocked over by two cats fighting ; a third is about to join in the fray.

Formerly attributed to Snyders.

Collection—Sir Thomas Baring. Bought from Mr. Yates.
Bought, June 3, 1848, No. 74, £33, 2s.
Exhibited—British Institution, 1844, No. 55.

57   2. GAME.

Canvas. 26 × 35½ in.

On a stone step a brace of partridges, a hare, and some small birds. Behind them a hamper with a board lying across it, on which are a number of small birds.

Bought from Mr. Martin Colnaghi, 1867.

JAN GRIFFIER THE ELDER, 1645–1718.

58   1. LANDSCAPE.

Panel. 18½ × 24½ in.

A river running through a hilly country. On the left are booths with a number of figures. Beyond on a knoll is a large church, and farther off a rocky well-wooded hill, on the top of which is a large castle. In the foreground, on the extreme left sheltered by a tree, is an inn towards which several people are making their way. On the right is a château with a drawbridge, and a number of people on and near it. Beyond is a high hill on which stand a small church and some other buildings. On the river are several boats; on one of them is the signature.

Distant view in the centre; blue sky with light clouds.

59
2. LANDSCAPE.

Panel. 18½ × 24½ in.

The companion picture. A winding river opening out in the foreground, where are a number of boats with figures. On the bank, to the right, two quacks on a scaffold are addressing a crowd; behind them rises a rocky bank with cottages, trees, and a church. In the foreground, to the right, is a man fishing, another embracing a girl, and three more going through a low doorway leading up to a garden, where, beneath a trellis, are seated a fiddler and others. Farther off, on the bank of the river, are a number of mill-stones, one of which is being lowered by a crane into a boat. Beyond is a fortified headland. On the opposite bank, to the left, are people under some trees, a church, some cottages, and a castle. Distant landscape with hills to the left. Blue sky with clouds lighted by an evening sun. Signed on a boat in the front.

Collections—M. Peter Loquet, Amsterdam, Sold September 22, 1783, with the preceding picture, Nos. 115 and 116, 1000 florins to Van der Schley for M. Van Winter.
M. Van Loon.
Acquired by the Earl of Northbrook by exchange from Baron A. de Rothschild, 1880.

JAN HACKAERT, 1636–1699.

60
STARTING FOR THE CHASE.

Canvas. 26⅞ × 20⅞ in.

View in a wood at the Hague with a road leading from the middle distance on the left to the right foreground, enlivened with figures, probably by Adrian Van de Velde. In the foreground is a huntsman with three dogs, with a pike over his left shoulder and a horn slung at his side; a little behind him are a gentleman on a chestnut horse, and a lady on a white horse, the latter holding a hawk, with an attendant on foot behind them, a man with a frame of hawks, and three dogs. Farther off are two cavaliers, an attendant, and two dogs. Through the trees are seen glimpses of the distant landscape. Morning sky.

Bought from M. Nieuwenhuys, 1854.

FRANS HALS THE ELDER, 1584–1666.

61 PETER, SON OF CORNELIUS VAN DER MORSCH.

Panel, oak. 33¼ × 26½ in.

Portrait of a man in black with a white ruff. Half-length; the face, seen in three-quarters, turned to the left; grey hair, moustachio, and short beard; with his left arm he holds a basket containing herrings packed in straw; in his right hand he holds up a herring. Dark-green background. On the right are the words "WIE BEGEERT;" on the left, a shield, bearing a half unicorn argent issuing from the waves, and the date ÆTAT SVÆ 73, 1616.

Collection.—M. Van Tol, Leiden. Sold June 15, 1772, No. 8, 15 florins, to Mr. Delfos.
Bought from Mr. Martin Colnaghi, 1866.
A. Van der Willigen, *Les Artistes de Harlem*, Harlem, 1870, pp. 348, 349.
Photographed, *Northbrook Gallery*.

Another portrait of Peter Van der Morsch (panel, 35 × 10½ in.), by an unknown artist, is preserved in the Museum at Lieden, Catalogue of 1879, No. 1418. Below it are these verses :

"Gerechts Bood 'van mijn Stadt, en Rederijkers sot,
Een lid der Akoley, daar Liefde is 't Fondament
Een vrijer tachtig oud, die 't misdrijf heeft bespot.
'k Ben Piero L.N.N. tijd, God weet mijn levens ent."

This portrait was formerly in the Chamber of Rhetoric, "De witte Acolyen," at Lieden, but, on its dissolution in 1734, it became the property of the town. Peter Van der Morsch, as we learn from the above-quoted inscription, and from various entries in the accounts of the town, was the official messenger of the Corporation, and also a member of the Chamber of Rhetoric. He was commonly known amongst his fellow-townsmen as Piero.

A drawing after the portrait by Hals, executed in the eighteenth century by Vincent Van der Vinne of Harlem, is now in the possession of M. Wertheim at Amsterdam. For the knowledge of this we are indebted to the late Mr. Ad. de Vries, assistant keeper of prints, &c., at the Museum of Amsterdam.

MEINDERT HOBBEMA, 1638–1709.

62   LANDSCAPE.

Panel, oak.   13 × 15 in.

A landscape divided by a river flowing across it, on which is a boat with a man rowing two gentlemen.   In the foreground, on the right, are some logs of timber, and beyond the stream a thick bank of trees, with their deep shade offering a charming contrast to the sunlit view on the left, with a church tower in the distance.   Blue sky, with a few light clouds.   Signed in the centre of the foreground.

Collections—M. Henry Muilman, Lord of Haamstede, Amsterdam. Sold April 12, 1813, No. 63, 640 florins, to Mr. T. T. Cremer.
M. Thomas Theodore Cremer, Rotterdam. Sold April 16, 1816, No. 35, 1300 florins, to M. Van Os.
Bought in Holland through Mr. Chaplin, 1847.
Smith, vi. 126, No. 42.
Waagen, *Treasures*, ii. 187.
Kugler, *Handbook*, ii. 478.

MELCHIOR D'HONDEKOETER, 1636–1695.

63   POULTRY.

Canvas.   31 × 39½ in.

In the middle, turned towards the left, a cock lifting up one foot; at his side, a hen feeding with four chickens, and in the foreground two more.   On the right a white hen resting, and in front another chick.   In the background, on the right, palings with a pigeon on the top, and trees beyond.   On the left, a landscape with fowls.   Signed on the wood : M DHONDEKOETER.

Bought from Mr. C. Annoot from a private collection near the Hague, 1865.

PHILIP KONINCK, 1619–1689.

64 LANDSCAPE IN GELDERLAND.

Canvas. 39 × 57¼ in.

An extensive landscape in Gelderland, with a river crossed by a bridge in the mid-distance. Beyond is woody scenery with villages, churches, windmills, and a distant town. In the foreground, on the left, is a cottage, before which is a woman feeding chickens; beyond, a church and some cottages embowered in trees. On the roadside are three labourers resting, and, coming down the road towards them, a cart laden with hay, followed by peasants and horsemen with dogs. Another cart is standing at a wayside inn in the centre, the driver attending to the horse, which is drinking at a trough; at the door is a man talking to the host, while a third is seated on a bench outside. In the foreground is a man with a dog, and on the right some sheep and a white horse. Blue sky with clouds. The figures by Adrian Van de Velde.

Collections—Sir Charles Bagot. Sold June 18, 1836, No. 35, £143, 17s, to
Mr. Brondgeest.
Verstolk.
Bought in 1846.
Exhibited—British Institution, 1850, No. 47.

SOLOMON KONINCK, 1609–166..

65 PORTRAIT.

Canvas. 26½ × 22½ in.

Bust of a man, life-size, grey hair. Fur dress with a gold chain.

Collection—Verstolk.
Bought in 1846.
Bürger, 253. "Peinture magistrale et digne de Rembrandt."

PETER JOSEPH LA FONTAINE, 1758-1835.

66   INTERIOR OF A CHURCH.

Panel.   6¾ × 9¼ in.

Interior of a five-aisled apsidal church, the choir-screen surmounted by a rood with statues of the Virgin and St. John. There are altars against the two easternmost pillars that separate the nave from the south aisle. In the north aisle is a singers' gallery vaulted beneath. A tablet against a pillar bears the signature :

> " P lafo
> ntaine
> fecit."

Collection—Mr. Samuel Rogers.
Bought, May 2, 1856, No. 532, £16, 5s., as by P. Neefs.

C. LELIENBERG, c. 1605-1660.

67   1. RABBIT-HUNTING.

Canvas.   42 × 49¾ in.

A tree with a trophy of game in the centre. Five spaniels chasing a rabbit to the right.

68 2. HARE-HUNTING.

Canvas. 42 × 49¾ in.

The companion picture. A tree with a trophy of game in the centre. Three dogs chasing a hare to the left.

Bought by the Earl of Northbrook from Messrs. Colnaghi, 1882.

--- —

JOHANN LINGELBACH, 1625-1687.

69 ITALIAN LANDSCAPE WITH PEASANTS.

Canvas. 42¾ × 35½ in.

On the left a tavern, with a canvas awning spread across from the house to an old tree in the centre. Underneath a number of persons are sitting enjoying themselves, and two men playing the bagpipes. In the centre a couple are dancing to the music. In front, on the right, is a man resting beside a well, and two dogs. Background of woody hills.

Collections—M. Van de Pot, Rotterdam.
            Verstolk.
Bought in 1846.
Waagen, *Treasures*, ii. 186. "Of rare delicacy of tone for this master, and very careful execution."

NICHOLAS MAAS, 1632–1693.

70   THE TIRED NURSE.

Panel. 18½ × 23 in.

A woman asleep, her head resting on a red cushion placed on the hood of a wicker-cradle in which a baby lies asleep. She wears a brown jacket, scarlet skirt, greenish-blue apron, white cap and tippet. and has a knife in her right hand, which rests on her lap, beside some apples. In the background are a chair, a table, and a window, through which are seen the roofs of some houses and a church tower.

This picture, in his earlier Rembrandtesque manner, with much body, is remarkable for the intensity of its colour.

Signed on the left in front, with the date, 1655.

Collection—M. Artaria.
Bought at his sale, 1850, £73, 10s.
Waagen, *Treasures*, ii. 183.
Viardot, 155.

FRANS VAN MIERIS THE ELDER, 1635–1681.

71   1. PORTRAIT OF THE ARTIST.

Panel, oval. 5½ × 4½ in.

Half-length, dressed in black, with a large turned-down collar; long hair and a slight moustachio. In his left hand he holds his palette and brushes. In the background, to the right, stands an easel.

Collections—Gerard Braamcamp, Amsterdam. Sold July 31, 1771, No. 137,
    100 florins, to J. Van den Berg.
   Lord Powerscourt.
Bought by the Earl of Northbrook, 1878.

72   2. THE MUSICAL LADY.

Panel. 9¾ × 7⅞ in.

A lady, in a light-coloured jacket with slashed sleeves, and a white satin skirt, is sitting holding a music-book, and leaning on a table, on which lies a lute, with two sets of tuning pegs, the lower containing fourteen and the higher eight; the thick table-cover, of a Turkey pattern, is pushed back. Architectural background, with a female statue (Flora ?) in a niche.

Collection—M. Trouart, Paris. Sold February 22, 1779, 730 francs.
Bought from M. Nieuwenhuys, 1850.
Smith, i. 71, No. 35.
Waagen, *Treasures*, ii. 183. "Of the painter's best period, most harmonious in colouring, and of wonderful precision of execution."

WILLEM VAN MIERIS, 1662-1747.

73   THE LETTER RECEIVED.

Panel. 15 × 12⅜ in.

At an arched opening, with a crimson curtain looped up on the right, a lady is sitting in a light-blue silk dress with slashed sleeves and a yellow velvet scarf. She stretches out her right arm towards an old woman, who stands behind her leaning on a stick, while she presents a letter, addressed "Juff⁵ me juff. Clara van Ha . . . de Heere . . . tot Amsterdam." On the carpet-covered table are two music-books, a guitar, and a dish of cherries, on which a parakeet, at the door of its open cage, is feasting. In the background is a green-curtained bedstead.

Bought in Holland through Mr. Chaplin, 1850.
Waagen, *Treasures*, ii. 183. "Of the master's best time."
Kugler, *Handbook*, ii. 513.
Photographed, *Northbrook Gallery.*

GABRIEL METSU, 1630–1668.

74

1. THE INTRUDER.

Panel, oak. 26 × 23¼ in.

The interior of a bed-chamber, hung with gilt leather, in which two ladies dressing are surprised by a young gentleman whom their maid is trying to hold back.   One of the ladies, wearing a green velvet jacket bordered with ermine, is sitting by the side of a table to the left with a comb in her hand, laughing.   The other stands by the side of a bed, from which she has apparently just risen, and looks offended.   On a chair to the right hangs an embroidered scarlet cloak trimmed with ermine.   On the left is a brown spaniel, and on the right, on the ground, a jug and a candlestick.

Signed on the woodwork of the bedstead.

Collections—Colonel Way. Sold to Messrs. Smith, by whom it was sold in 1830 to the Hon. G. F. Vernon for £525.

      Hon. G. F. Vernon. Sold April 15, 1831, No. 50, £403, 4s., to Messrs. Smith.

      Sir Charles Bagot. Sold June 18, 1836, No. 56, £615, to Mr. Brondgeest.

      Verstolk.

Bought in 1846.

Smith, iv. 102, No. 94, and ix. 524, No. 29.

Waagen, *Treasures*, ii. 183, "The liveliness of the scene, the sustained execution, the delicacy of aerial perspective, and the warm and transparent colouring, show this to be one of the *chefs-d'œuvre* of the Master, of his best middle period.

Kugler, *Handbook*, ii. 399.

Burger, 275, 276.

Viardot, 155.

Exhibited—Manchester, 1857, No. 1059.

      Royal Academy, 1871, No. 211 ; and 1880, No. 128.

75

2. PORTRAIT OF THE ARTIST.

Panel, oak. $6\frac{3}{8} \times 5\frac{1}{4}$ in.

About forty years of age, half-length, turned to the right, the face seen in three-quarters, dressed in a brown coat, a white cravat, and white wrist-bands, with a cap lined with white on his head; he wears his hair long, and has a short mustachio. He is smoking a long clay pipe held in his right hand.

Signed above on the right.

Collections—Lambert-Witsen, Amsterdam. Sold May 25, 1746, No. 6, 40 florins, to G. Braamcamp.
Gerard Braamcamp, Amsterdam. Sold July 31, 1771, No. 133, 102 florins, to C. Ploos van Amstal.
Sir Charles Bagot. Sold June 18, 1836, No. 28, £55, 13s., to Mr. Brondgeest.
Verstolk.

Bought in 1846.

Smith, iv. 82, No. 28, and ix. 518, No. 8. "This interesting picture is painted with great breadth and masterly effect."

76

3. CHILD ASLEEP.

Panel, oak. $5\frac{3}{8} \times 5\frac{1}{4}$ in.

Portrait of a pale child with light hair, lying asleep in bed. The head only seen.

Collections—Dr. Charles Chauncey.
Mr. C. Baring Wall.

PETER NEEFS, 1570–1651.

77   INTERIOR OF A CHURCH.

Copper.   7¼ × 9½ in.

Interior of a three-aisled, cruciform church, taken from the west
end of the nave. The apsidal choir is separated from the body of the
building by a screen, the high altar being seen through the open
central gates. The organ is on the south, over the entrance of the
ambulatory. Above the intersection of the nave and transept is a
lantern. Altars with triptychs are placed against three of the
cylindrical columns that separate the nave from the south aisle; at
the westernmost of these a priest is saying mass, at which an acolyte
and seven people are assisting. A small pulpit with a sounding-
board stands against one of the columns on the north side; at the
foot of the westernmost column on this side is seated a cripple; above
him is a tablet on which the artist's name is inscribed, with the date,
16 . . There are altogether twenty five figures and three dogs in
the picture.

Collection—Mr. Samuel Rogers.
Bought, May 2, 1856, No. 533, £21.

CASPAR NETSCHER, 1639–1684.

78   A GIRL.

Panel. 13¼ × 10¼ in.

Portrait of a little girl, with light hair in ringlets, sitting on a stone table, which is partly covered by a carpet. She is dressed in white satin, with a string of pearls round her neck and pearl earrings. In her lap is a bunch of grapes, and she is taking some more from a plate held by her nurse, who is standing behind her. To the right is a crimson curtain, and to the left a balustrade, with a view of trees behind. On the back is an inscription, partly effaced : JOHANNES H.

Collections—Admiral Lord Radstock. Sold May 13, 1826, No. 19, £79, 16s., to Mr. Hollingsworth.
    Mr. John Slater. Sold April 22, 1837, No. 78, £78, 15s., to Mr. Kermann.
    Mr. William Wells.
Bought, May 13, 1848, No. 78, £111, 6s.
Smith, iv. 159, No. 46. "This exquisitely-painted picture was sold in a collection in Paris for 5000 francs (£200)."
Waagen, *Treasures,* ii. 183.
Kugler, *Handbook,* ii. 400.

79   2. PORTRAIT.

Panel. 14½ × 10¼ in.

Three-quarter length. A gentleman stands turned to the right, his left hand open, and his right on his chest. He wears his hair long, has a reddish-brown dress, a long, white muslin cravat, and full white shirt-sleeves. On the left is a red curtain looped up; on the right, through an open window, a garden with large pots of flowers and trees.

Signed on the window-sill, with the date 1680.

Collections—Sir Thomas Baring. Sold June 3, 1848, No. 78, £6, 6s.
    Sir Francis T. Baring (Lord Northbrook).

80   3. THE DUCHESS OF MAINE.

Panel, rounded top. 13½ × 10 in.

Full-length portrait of a lady of rank, with a high lace head-dress, standing, turned to the right, in the angle of a terrace, the face seen in full. She is holding up the skirt of her crimson velvet dress with her right hand, and her left rests on the parapet, close to a basket of fruit and flowers, of which she holds a spray. On the ground are more flowers and fruit. On the lady's right, a macaw.

Collection—Mr. Ralph Bernal.
Bought, March 10, 1855, No. 651, £30, 0s.
In the catalogue the lady is described as "the Duchess of Burgundy."

PAUL POTTER, 1625–1654.

81   THE YOUNG BULL.

Panel. 21½ × 26 in.

Side view of a young reddish-brown bull, with two sheep lying under a tree on the left, and a frog in the foreground. There is a meadow with cattle in the middle distance, and a village in the distance towards the centre. Cloudy sky, very dark near the horizon to the right. Signed on the right, with the date 1647.

Collections—M. Proley. Sold 1786, 4376 francs.
      Mr. Edward Gray.
      Sir Thomas Baring.
Bought, June 3, 1848, No. 131, £220, 10s.
Smith, v. 135, No. 36.
Waagen, *Treasures*, ii. 185. "The masterly manner in which the animal is painted, and the general energetic treatment, brings this picture very near to the celebrated Young Bull at the Hague."
T. Van Westrheene, *Paulus Potter*, La Haye, 1867, p. 150, No. 43.
Exhibited—Royal Academy, 1871, No. 172.

ADAM PYNACKER, 1621–1673.

82   1. LANDSCAPE.

Canvas. 16½ × 17 in.

A rocky height on the left, connected with a town gate on the
right by an arch thrown across a gorge, with a river below. On the
bridge are peasants and donkeys. Below, in the foreground on the
left, a peasant with cattle, a goat, and sheep coming out from an
archway in the rocks. In the distance a blue mountain. Clear
evening sky. Signed.

Collection—M. Artaria.
Bought at his sale, 1850, £41, 18s.
Waagen, *Treasures*, ii. 187. "An admirable specimen of this unequal master."
Kugler, *Handbook*, ii. 490.

83   2. LANDSCAPE.

Canvas. 21¼ × 18 in.

View up a mountain valley, with cottages, and in the distance a
high mountain. On the left a torrent falls in a cascade in the foreground. Up the valley, in mid-distance, the roadway is formed by
a viaduct of logs; at its farther end is a man on a donkey, another
driving a couple of oxen, and a flock of goats. On the right are
trees and the sloping side of a mountain. In the foreground a
peasant woman on a donkey, followed by another with packages, is
crossing a wooden bridge. Signed to the left of the centre.

Collection—Earl of Beverley.
Bought in 1851.

REMBRANDT VAN RYN, 1607–1669.

84   ADORATION OF THE MAGI.

Panel.   47 × 40 in.

On the left, in the open air, the Virgin, seated, holds the infant Jesus. At his feet a King kneeling, with two persons behind him, presents his offering, on the ground before him lies his turban. Behind the Child another King, in a very rich costume, is taking from the hands of an attendant the presents he is about to offer. On the right a third King, wearing his crown, holds a sceptre in his left hand; to his right is a man holding a turban in his left and a censer in his right hand; these two wear red Turkish boots. In the centre of the composition, in the half distance, a King wearing a turban stands leaning with his left hand on a staff. Behind him an umbrella, and a camel accompanied by three men. On the right of this King is an attendant, and in the background are two more figures. On the left the cottage, with Joseph, and above its roof the star.

Painted in brown with a very little colour. Signed to the left, with the date 1659.

85   2. PORTRAIT.

Panel.   26¼ × 22½ in.

Bust of an old man, life-size. He wears a velvet cap and a cloak
with a jewelled clasp. With his right hand he grasps the jewelled
handle of a staff. Signed, with the date 1667.

Collections—Mr. Emmerson.
                    Verstolk.
Bought in 1846.
Waagen, *Galleries*, 98.

86   3. LANDSCAPE.

Panel.   11¼ × 8¼ in.

A stream crossed by a bridge, with a road leading up to it from
the right; on the road are a coach drawn by four grey horses, a man
and a dog. The sky is dark with heavy rain-clouds, leaving in light
only the centre of the middle distance and the left background, where
there is a town with high buildings and a windmill. Landscapes
by this master are rare; into them, as here, he always introduces
coaches.

Collection—Catalogue of pictures on sale at Mr. Woolburn's, No. 54.
Bought of M. Nieuwenhuys, 1854.
Exhibited—British Institution, 1843, No. 66; and Royal Academy, 1880,
No. 118.
Waagen, *Galleries*, 98. "Highly poetical and melancholy in feeling, and of
great power and depth of chiaroscuro."

PETER PAUL RUBENS, 1577–1640.

87   1. ABRAHAM AND MELCHISEDECH.

Panel, oak. 26¼ × 32¼ in.

A composition of about twenty figures, in the centre of which
Abraham, bareheaded, clad in armour, and wearing a crimson mantle,
advances up a step towards Melchisedech, who presents him with
two loaves. Melchisedech wears a crown of olive and a yellow robe
lined with ermine, the train of which is held by a page. Behind
him stands a man with a basket of bread on his back, and on his
right are four persons, two of whom are distributing bread to some
soldiers. Behind these, on the left, are two more soldiers, and a
youth holding Abraham's horse. In the immediate foreground, on
the right, are two men with pots of wine. The subject is enclosed
within an architectural frame consisting of a cornice supported by
pillars, to which three cherubs are attaching drapery, one end of
which hangs down on the left, and lies on the pavement across the
front.

Collections—Said to have come from the Palazzo Nuovo at Madrid.
         M. Julienne, Paris. Sold March 30, 1767, No. 98, 3840 francs.
         John Lord Trevor's widow, 1782.
         Lady Stepney. Put up May 1, 1830, No. 93 ; bought in, £64.
         Hon. Lady Stuart. Sold 1841, £598, 10s.
         M. Nieuwenhuys.
         Sir Thomas Baring.
Bought, June 3, 1848, No. 121, £383, 5s.

The following probably refer to another, or to other pictures.
1825, 7th May. Collection of Simon M'Gillivray, Esq.—No. 25. Abraham, on his
return from conquest, offering tithes to Melchisedech; a sketch of the great picture in
the Earl of Grosvenor's collection. Painted with force and spirit. £12, 12s., to Mr.
Dyson. Resold on 18th June for £8, 6s. to Mr. Crawford.
1833, 2nd March. Collection imported from Westphalia by Mr. Mertens.—No. 47,
£54, 12s., to Davis.

Exhibited—British Institution, 1841, No. 69.
Smith, ii. 184, No. 641, ix. 323, No. 288. "A finished study of superlative
excellence for the large picture in the collection of Earl Grosvenor."
Waagen, Treasures, ii. 182.

88   2. THE WAGGON.

Panel, oak.   19¾ × 21¾ in.

View in a wooded country crossed by a stream.   On the right is a
waggon drawn by two horses, one of which, ridden by the driver in
red, is going down a steep bank to the water.   On the other side of
the stream is a clump of trees.   Another clump fills the centre.   The
scene is lighted up by the setting sun.*

Collections—Mr. R. Reinagle. Sold May 29, 1824, No. 16, £21, to Mr. D.
            Ring.
            Earl of Mulgrave. Sold May 12, 1832, No. 18, £43, 1s., to Mr.
            Swaby.
            Marquis of Camden. Sold 1841, £288, 15s.
            Mr. Samuel Rogers.
Bought, May 3, 1856, No. 717, £640, 10s.
Smith, ix. 331, No. 322.
Waagen, Galleries, 98.
Viardot, 155.
Exhibited—British Institution, 1850, No. 28.
            Royal Academy, 1872, No. 51.

   * There is a copy of this fine sketch in the National Gallery. Wynn Ellis's Collection,
No. 948.   Panel, 18½ × 23 in.

JACOB RUISDAEL, 1825–1682.

89   1. CASTLE OF BREDEVODE.

Panel.   15½ × 16 in.

A shallow piece of water with an oak and other trees on the right,
among which is a man in a scarlet jacket fishing.   To the left, a
portion of the ruins of the Castle of Bredevode with a wood beyond.
Evening light with a clouded sky.   Signed on the left with the
cipher.

Collection—Duc de Berri. Exhibited for sale at Christie's in 1834, and priced
£160.
Bought through Mr. Chaplin, 1848.
Smith, vi. 80, No. 255.
Waagen, Treasures, ii. 167.
Exhibited—Royal Academy, 1872, No. 184.

90   2. WINDMILL.

Panel.   12¼ × 17¾ in.

In the foreground a river. On the right a shed; nearly in the
centre a windmill, with a man and woman near the door. On the
left, in the mid-distance, a church and an abbey in ruins. Beyond,
a line of low trees. Fresh morning light. Signed with initials on
the right.

Collection—Earl of Beverley.
Bought in 1851.
Smith, ix. 681, No. 3.
Waagen, *Galleries*, 99.
Exhibited—Royal Academy, 1872, No. 167.

91   3. WATERFALL.

Canvas.   18¼ × 16 in.

A landscape with a waterfall in the foreground. On the left, a
wooded bank with a few fir trees, and on the height a man drawing,
and another leaning on a stick looking on. On the right, a cottage
with trees and sheep. In the centre, distant hills, over which a
cloud is lighted by the sun. Signed on the left.

Collection—King of Holland. Sold August 12, 1850, No. 95, 920 florins, to
M. Nieuwenhuys.
Bought from M. Nieuwenhuys, 1851.
Waagen, *Galleries*, 99.
Exhibited—Royal Academy, 1872, No. 206.

92   4. CORNFIELDS.

Canvas. 18 × 22 in.

An upland landscape with cornfields, cottages, and trees. Near the front is a man with a pole on his left shoulder going towards the left with two dogs before him. In the mid-distance, two men conversing over a hedge. Blue sky with fleecy clouds. Signed to the left of the centre.

Collection—Mr. Hope, Paris.
Bought through Mr. Smith, 1849.
Waagen, *Treasures*, ii. 187. "Besides the usual Ruisdael attractions, this picture exhibits an uncommon lightness of tone, while the tender, airy clouds show the influence of his great contemporary Hobbema."
Revoil, *Une Visite à la National Gallery*, Paris, 1878, 2nd partie, p. 73.
Exhibited—British Institution, 1850, No. 143.
       Royal Academy, 1871, No. 198, and 1880, No. 121.

93   5. BLEACHING GROUND.

Canvas. 14½ × 18 in.

View of the plain before Haarlem, with some cottages on the left, and a bleaching-ground, on which a gleam of sunshine falls, extending across the picture. The mid-distance is wooded, with several houses among the trees. In the distance, on the right, is seen the town with its church, and short slender central turret. Blue sky with light clouds. Signed in the right corner.

Collection—Earl of Beverley.
Bought in 1851.
Smith, ix. 683, No. 7.
Waagen, *Galleries*, 90. "This picture takes a high place among this class of Ruisdael's works. It possesses great truth of effect, and the execution, though careful, is free and spirited."
Exhibited—Royal Academy, 1872, No. 205.

94   6. A FRESH BREEZE.

Canvas. 25 × 31¾ in.

View on the Y off Amsterdam, with a flat coast stretching across the background. A brisk wind from the left is driving some fishing-craft before it. One of them, near the centre, scudding under a white mainsail, has a small boat attached to her stern; another, with a red sail, is tacking. Here and there are breaks in the dark clouds, with glimpses of blue sky. In the front, on the right, is a break-water of piles. The town is seen in the distance on the left. Signed in the right corner.

Collection—Earl of Beverley.
Bought in 1851.
Smith, ix. 681, No. 2.
Waagen, *Treasures*, II. 187.
Viardot, 155, who writes of this picture and the Cuyp (No. 44): "Ces deux *Marines* des deux illustres rivaux ont à elles seules la valeur d'une galerie, et méritent l'hommage de tout ami des arts."
Exhibited—Royal Academy, 1871, No. 224.

GODEFRIED SCHALCKEN, 1643-1706.

95   PORTRAIT OF DE WITT.

Copper. 16¾ × 13 in.

The Grand Pensioner is represented facing the spectator, slightly turned to the right. He wears a black silk robe and white collar; his right arm rests on a table, and his left hand, which is gloved, is on his hip. He has long, flowing grey hair, which falls on his shoulders. In the background is a crimson curtain, through which are seen some buildings. Signed on the right, below.

An admirable portrait of the painter's best time, carefully and delicately painted, with more animation than usual.

Collections—A collection in Amsterdam.
           Verstolk.
Bought in 1846.
Smith, ix, 590, No. 9.
Waagen, *Treasures*, ii. 183.
Photographed, *Northbrook Gallery*.

HENDRIK MARTENZ SORG, 1621-1682.

96   FISH MARKET.

Panel. 12 × 10 in.

A fish market with nine figures, those in the foreground three-quarter length. In the front are fish exposed for sale on a stall, behind which, on the loft, stands a sturdy fishwoman in a red jacket, bluish green cape, and a hat, holding in her right hand a chopper. She is putting the head of a cod into a flat basket held by a boy standing opposite. A gentleman is leaning forward and paying for his purchases. In the background are other figures, and the masts and sails of two fishing-smacks. Behind is a building with a small round-headed opening, the shutter of which is closed and secured by a lock. Over it the date: 1655.

Collection—M. John van der Linden van Slingeland, Dordrecht. Sold August 22, 1785, No. 392, 105 florins, to Mr. Muys.
Bought from M. Nieuwenhuys, 1854.

JAN STEEN, 1626–1679.

97   1. PORTRAIT OF THE ARTIST.

Panel. $21\frac{3}{4} \times 16\frac{1}{2}$ in.

About forty years of age, three-quarters face, turned to the right. He sits on a rush-bottomed chair, his right leg placed on his left knee, playing on a lute which he is accompanying with his voice, the drollery of his song being unmistakably indicated by the expression of his face. He wears a yellow dress, greenish slashed hose, and a dark red cap; a brown mantle lined with red hangs from his shoulders over the back of his chair. Upon a table, on the right, are some music-books and a metal tankard. A large green curtain hangs behind him. A spirited picture, of masterly execution, painted in delicate, broken tones, with great transparency. Lighted from the front on the left. Signed on the right.*

Engraved by G. W. Marr, 1832, as frontispiece of Part IV. of Smith's "Catalogue Raisonné;" $5\frac{1}{4} \times 4\frac{3}{4}$ in.
Engraved, mezzotint, by John Cole of Amsterdam, with the inscription, "Ad se ipsum pinxit."
Collections—M. Joseph A. Brentano, Amsterdam. Sold May 13, 1822, No. 324, 295 florins, to Mr. Brondgeest.
　　　　　Verstolk.
Bought in 1846.
Smith, iv. 39, No. 121.
Waagen, *Treasures*, ii. 184.
Kugler, *Handbook*, ii. 403.
T. van Westrheene, *Jan Steen: Etude sur l'Art en Hollande.* La Haye, 1856, p. 114, No. 64.
Exhibited—Royal Academy, 1880, No. 77.

---

* Besides the portraits of Jan Steen described in Smith, there is a very characteristic half-length, life size, at Woburn Abbey. (Catalogue, No. 165.)

98   2. THE DOCTOR.

Panel. 23½ × 19½ in.

A bedroom, in the middle of which stands the doctor, dressed in black, with a frilled collar and wristbands and a high hat, writing a prescription for a young woman who lies in a bed with brown curtains on the right. On the right of the doctor an old woman looks at him with a grin; behind her is an anxious-looking old man, and at her side a boy. The end of the table is covered with a green cloth, on which stands a coffee-pot. Through the open door is seen a young man apparently about to come in. Signed on a piece of paper lying on the floor to the right.

Etched by A. Brondgeest.
Collections—M. Isaac Hoogenbergh, Amsterdam. Sold April 10, 1743, No. 38, 150 florins. (It is doubtful whether this is the same picture.)
         M. Van Noort, Château of Ter Wadding, near Leiden. Sold April 29, 1845, for 1400 florins, by private contract, to Baron Verstolk.
    Verstolk.
Bought in 1846.
Smith, ix. 476, No. 9. "Merits the warmest commendation."
Waagen, *Treasures*, ii. 184.
Vinrdot, 155.
T. van Westrheene, *Jan Steen*, 115, No. 60.
Exhibited—Royal Academy, 1870, No. 15, and 1889, No. 80.

99   3. SCHOOL IN AN UPROAR.

Panel.   15 × 19¼ in.

A set of mischievous scholars are playing tricks while their old fat
schoolmaster is fast asleep. One has put on his spectacles, another
is playing the flute, and a third has brought in a pig, which is
eating up the exercises. Signed to the left, with the date 1672.

Collections—M. Peter Cuauw, Leiden. Sold August 12, 1708, 115 florins.
          A Collection in Amsterdam. Sold for 1600 florins to Baron
                  Verstolk.
          Verstolk.
Bought in 1846.
Smith, iv. 46, No. 140.
Waagen, *Treasures*, ii. 184. " A charming picture, both for the humour of the
          subject and the spirit of the treatment. '
Kugler, *Handbook*, ii. 403.
T. van Westrheene, *Jan Steen*, 115, No. 67.
Exhibited— Manchester, 1857, No. 1051.

DAVID TENIERS I., 1582–1649.

100   1. THE FORTUNE-TELLER.

Panel, oak. 6¾ × 10 in.

On a rising knoll, in the centre, a peasant holds out his hand to a gipsy who is telling him his fortune. On the ground, by her side, is a basket with linen. At the foot of some rocks, on the right, are two gipsy women, seated. On the other side of a valley, on the left, a cottage stands at the foot of a wooded hill. A little bit of distant landscape is seen in the centre of the background.

Signed, on the right, with initials.

Collection—Sir Thomas Baring.
Bought, June 3, 1848, No. 77, £21.

101   2. LANDSCAPE.

Panel, oak. 25¼ × 35¼ in.

On the right is a house by a stream with a high bridge leading to its door, at which a man is standing bidding farewell to a young man and woman. In the foreground, on a road beside the stream, are four men. On the left there are hills and a church in the distance. Cloudy sky, with rays of light from the left. Signed with initials.

Collection—Earl of Beverley.
Bought in 1851.

DAVID TENIERS II., 1610–1690.

102 1. CORPS DE GARDE.

Copper. $15\frac{1}{2} \times 19\frac{3}{4}$ in.

A youth in green with long hair is hanging up a pair of pistols in holsters; on the ground lie a saddle, a cuirass, and other pieces of armour. A pair of gauntlets and a plumed helmet are on a table to the left. In the room behind a man stands before the fire with a pipe in his hand, and four others are sitting at a table, two of them playing at cards. A woman is coming in at a side door on the right. In the foreground to the right a sword rests against a stool. There is a broken pipe on the ground, and near it the signature. Over the chimney is a drawing on paper of a man's head with the date 1647.

Collections—Benjamin da Costa, the Hague. Sold August 13, 1764, No. 69, 610 florins, the companion, No. 70, 645 florins. The pair were subsequently sold to Mr. Braamcamp for 730 florins.

Gerard Braamcamp, Amsterdam. Sold July 31, 1771, No. 220, 1140 florins.

Peter Locquet. Sold September 23, 1783, No. 350, 1100 florins.

M. Van Leyden. Sold 1804, No. 86, 3100 francs, to Mr. Martin.

M. David, London. Put up July 17, 1819, No. 49; bought in at £278, 5s.

M. David, London. Sold May 27, 1820, No. 111, £162, 15s., to M. Bonnemaison.

M. Lapeyrière, Paris. Sold April 21, 1825, 12,990 francs.

Mr. Walsh Porter. Sold May 6, 1826, £407, 8s.

Mr. Joseph Barchard. Sold 1826, £404, 5s.

M. de la Bruyere.

Prince de Beauveau.

Bought through Mr. Chaplin, 1848.

De Bastide, *La Temple des Arts, ou le Cabinet de M. Braamcamp*, Amsterdam, 1766, p. 61.

Smith, iii. 300, No. 145.

Nieuwenhuys, *Review*, 238.

Waagen, *Treasures*, ii. 184. "This picture, in point of unrivalled beauty of treatment, in the cool tones and bold and almost plastic modelling, may be considered one of his *chefs-d'œuvre*."

Exhibited—Royal Academy, 1872, No. 186.

103   2. THE PHILOSOPHER.

Panel, oak. 16¾ × 14¼ in.

A grey-bearded old man, holding a paper in his left hand and a
pair of eye-glasses in his right, is seated in a high-backed chair
before a table on the left of the picture. He wears a blueish
robe and cap bordered with brown fur. On the table, which is
covered with a blueish-green cloth, are a globe, a skull, an hour-
glass, a large open book, a closed one, and an inkstand. Behind the
man, on the left, is an arm-chair, and further back a stick leaning
against the grey wall which forms the background; to this wall, on
the extreme right, is fastened a drawing on paper representing the
bust of a youth, dated 164 . On the right is a shelf with a bottle
and a box on it, and a wallet suspended beneath.

Collection—Earl of Beverley.
Bought in 1851.
Smith, ix. 444, No. 116. "A good picture."

104   3. PEASANTS DRINKING.

Panel, oak. 9¾ × 6¾ in.

In the centre, a young man in a yellow jacket and blue hose is
sitting on a cask holding a brown jug in one hand and a glass of
liquor in the other. To his left is a larger cask with a linen cloth
and a pan of charcoal on it. On the cask leans a man in a grey
jacket and scarlet cap, with a pipe in his right hand which he has
just taken out of his mouth whence he is puffing smoke. Behind
stands another man in brown filling his pipe, and on the right a
fourth, his face turned towards the wall which forms the background.
Signed on the left.

Collection—Earl of Beverley.
Bought in 1851.
Smith, ix. 445, No. 118.

105   4. VILLAGE FESTIVAL.

Panel, oak. 10¾ × 14½ in.

A composition of about forty figures assembled in front of an inn
with a lean-to shed on the left. In the centre a young man and
woman are dancing to the music of a bagpipe played by a man sitting
on a barrel; two other men are trying to persuade an oldish woman
to dance; others are drinking and talking. On the right are a
couple seated, and a man leaning against a fence; his pipe, the
tobacco still alight, lies on the ground. In the centre is a little dog.
Beyond is some rising ground, with figures on a winding road; in
the distance a village church. Signed on the left.

This celebrated picture, one of the best of its class, has been
engraved. It is, as Dr. Waagen well observes, remarkable for its
"richness of composition, happily conceived motives, transparency
and warmth of colouring, and spirited treatment."

On the back of the panel are the arms of Queen Elizabeth of
Bourbon.

Collections—Royal Collection, Madrid.
            Duchess de Berri.
            Marquis de Montcalm.
Bought at his sale, 1849, £283, 10s.
Waagen, *Treasures*, ii. 184.
Exhibited—Manchester, 1857, No. 1006.

106   5. BARGAINING FOR PIGS.

Panel, oak.   18½ × 27 in.

In the centre of an enclosed court which occupies the foreground
are three men, one of whom, in a grey jacket, is raising his right
hand as if to conclude a bargain by striking the palm of another,
dressed in a suit of black.   The third, an older man, is leaning on a
stick between them.   On the left is seen the subject of the bargain,
nine pigs, one of which is squealing as the boy who holds its ear fast
turns round to listen to what is passing.   Just within the cottage
door is a woman, while up above, at the granary window, the shutter
of which is thrown open, is an old man looking down.   The yard is
shut in to the right by wooden palings, beyond which are two or
three trees.   On the ground, to the right, are three red earthenware
pans.   Blue sky with grey clouds.   Painted in a clear, silvery tone.
Signed on the left.

Collection—Earl of Beverley.
Bought in 1851.
Smith, ix. 461, No. 172.
Viardot, 155.
Exhibited—Royal Academy, 1872, No. 161.

107   6. LANDSCAPE.

Panel, oak.   17¾ × 28½ in.

On the left, a large thatched house, outside which are eight
men, three standing talking.   Close to the cottage, are five more
men.   From the granary window, the shutter of which stands open,
a man in a red cap is looking down, while at the door is seen
the back of a woman who is just entering the cottage.   In the foreground is a spaniel, and a little to the right of the centre a cauldron
and other kitchen utensils, some on a bench, the rest on the ground,
where are also lying a couple of mussel shells.

In the distance there is a village church embowered in trees, and a
hill with a windmill, and a cottage at its foot, near a winding stream,
on the further bank of which are some willows.   On the rising ground
beyond are some trees, and on the extreme right two cottages, in
front of which are some men.   Blue sky with clouds.   Signed close
to the kitchen utensils, in front.

The house seems to be the same as that in " Bargaining for Pigs,"
to which this picture is the companion.

Collection—Earl of Beverley.
Bought in 1851.
Smith, ix. 400, No. 171.

108   7. THE HARVEST.

Panel, oak.   14 × 21½ in.

A cornfield with peasants reaping, binding, and stacking. In the
foreground a group of labourers eating their dinner. A church and
some cottages with trees in the mid-distance. In the distance a
shower with gleams of sunshine, and part of a rainbow on the left.
Two magpies are crossing the centre of the sky. In the foreground,
on the right, is a plough, near which is the signature.

Engraved in reverse by James Philip le Bas, with the title "Moisson, ou III.
Vue de Flandre." 12⅞×17½ in.
Collections—Chevalier de la Roque, Paris. Sold 1745, 250 francs.
        Duc de Choiseul.
        M. de Castelmore. Sold December 20, 1791, 2396 francs.
Bought from M. Nieuwenhuys, 1850.
Smith, iii. 279, No. 63.
Waagen, Treasures, ii. 185. "This is one of the finest landscapes I know by
Teniers ; it exhibits a fresh and true feeling for nature."

109   8 and 9. DUCKS, &c. (a pair).

Panel, oak.   18 × 14¾ in.

A pool of water fringed with flags, bulrushes, and other aquatic
plants. Six ducks and four ducklings are on the water. Two other
ducks are flying away. A kingfisher sits on the branch of a tree, on
the left, and a stork on the right in the distance. At the foot of
some trees, on a steep bank on the left, are five rabbits. Signed, in
the foreground, on the right.

110

A little bay fringed with flags, bulrushes, and other aquatic plants. Six ducks and the same number of ducklings on the water. Another duck and a kingfisher flying away. On a hilly bank, crowned with trees, are four rabbits. Signed, in the foreground, on the right.

Engraved by James Philip le Bas. 14⅞ × 11⅞ in.
Collection—Lord Northwick. Sold at his sale by Phillips, August 11, 1859, Nos. 1056 and 1057, £94, 10s.
Bought from Mr. Smith, 1859.
Smith, iii. 415, Nos. 579 and 580.

111   10. MONKEYS AT CARDS.

Copper.   6¾ × 8½ in.

Two monkeys, one in a red mantle and cap with three feathers in it, the other dressed in blue, are playing cards. In the background, a third holds a stoneware jug with its right paw, and lifts up a glass of liquor with its left. On the right, a monkey in yellow, with a pipe in its left paw, puffs smoke from its mouth. A dark-grey wall in the background. Cards, money, and a piece of chalk lie on the ground near the front. Signed on the right.

Collection—Lord Amherst.
Bought through Mr. Chaplin, 1850.

112   11. MONKEYS SHAVING CATS.

Panel, oak.   6⅞ × 8⅞ in.

In the middle, a cat sitting on a stool, with a towel round its neck, is holding up a brass basin with its two fore paws. A monkey dressed in blue, standing at the cat's side, has one paw on the top of its head, and with the other is lathering its face. To the left stands a brass vessel of hot water on an iron stand, and over it a white cloth.

To the right, another cat in a high-backed chair is holding a mirror, while a monkey trims its moustachio. In the corner, a third monkey is heating curling-irons Background, a wall with a shelf, on which are various utensils, and a sheet of paper with a drawing—apparently a Flemish rebus—on it. Signed in the right corner.

Collection—Lord Amherst.
Bought through Mr. Chaplin, 1850.
Waagen, *Treasures,* ii. 165. " Full of humour and truth of nature, and painted with delicate silvery tones."

GERARD TER BURG, 1608–1681.

113   1. LADY DRINKING.

Panel. 17¼ × 13¾ in.

A young lady in a yellow jacket and a grey skirt, with a black silk mantle and cap, sits on a red leather chair turned to the right, the face seen in profile, the figure to the knees. In her right hand is a white stoneware jug which she rests on her knees; with her left she holds a glass of liquor to her lips. On a writing-table before her are a sheet of paper, partly written on, and an inkstand. In the background is a closely-curtained bed.

Collections—M. Blondel d'Azincourt, Paris. Sold February 10, 1783, No. 20, 1100 francs.
       M. Héris, Brussels.
       Verstolk.
Bought in 1846.
Smith, iv. 120, No. 27 ; ix. 533, No. 15.
Waagen, *Treasures*, ii. 183.

---

114   2. LADY WRITING.

Panel. 17 × 17¼ in.

A young lady with light hair and a fair complexion, in a low pink jacket and dark skirt, sits at a table writing a letter. She is turned to the left, the face seen in profile, the figure to the knees. On the table are an inkstand and a table-cover doubled up. In the background is a closely-curtained bed with brown drapery.

A picture nearly identical with this was sold in the Choiseul Collection (No. 59 of the illustrated catalogue) for 1500 francs. It passed into the collection of M. Six van Heligen of Amsterdam. A third is in the Belvidere Gallery, Vienna.

Collections—M. Héris, Brussels.
       Verstolk.
Bought in 1846.
Waagen, *Treasures*, ii. 183.

JAN VAN DE CAPELLE, c. 1630-c. 1685.

115   1. MOUTH OF THE BRILL.

Canvas. 28¼ × 37 in.

In the centre a Dutch dogger, with nine persons in it, is approaching, while a rowing-boat passes before it in which are four passengers, two gentlemen, a lady, and an officer in a red coat, who is saluting a gentleman in the other boat. Close to the bank on the left, on which is a tower, is another sailing vessel with a little boat at its stern. On the right is a jetty, on which are two men; beyond it, towards the open sea, a frigate and several vessels sailing in different directions. On a post on the right, in the foreground, is the signature I. V. CAPPELLE.

Painted in this master's best manner. The passing clouds throw a strong shadow on the water, as is often the case after a shower at sunset. Transparently executed in deep tones.

Collection—Lord Charles Townshend.
Nieuwenhuys, *Review*, 88.
Waagen, *Treasures*, ii. 188.

116   2. A CALM.

Canvas. 22¾ × 26 in.

A quiet sea with numerous boats. In the front a strip of beach. In the centre, a boy with a basket on his back is wading towards a boat run ashore. On the extreme right are sandhills, and beyond the buildings of a town. The sky is overcast. Strong shadows in the foreground.

Bought from Mr. Smith, 1847.
Waagen, *Treasures*, ii. 188.
Exhibited—Royal Academy, 1889, No. 122.

WILLEM VAN DE VELDE, 1633-1707.

117

1. VIEW ON A RIVER.

Canvas. 15 × 18½ in.

On the left, two coasters with people on board. In the centre, a six-oared boat, full of passengers, making for the shore. On the right, vessels at anchor. In the foreground to the right, a fisherman kneeling by a basket, and part of a boat, on which are the initials W. V. V.

Collection—Earl of Beverley.
Bought in 1851.
Smith, ix. 757, No. 1.

118

2. A CALM.

Canvas. 27 × 34 in.

On the left, a jetty, on which are a gentleman and two porters. Two coasters, with their colours (barry of six, *gules* and *argent*) flying and their sails hanging loose, are being made fast to the jetty. In the centre is a small rowboat, with four men in it, one of whom holds a rope, the other end of which is held by a man standing at the stern of the farther coaster. Beyond is a third vessel. On the right is a six-oared boat containing passengers, and farther off a frigate at anchor with a flag, *or*, a lion rampant *gules*, and the Dutch colours. Several other vessels receding in succession serve to complete the composition. Signed on the jetty with the date 1661.

Collections—Mr. Henry Muilman, Amsterdam. Sold April 13, 1813, No. 103, 1000 francs, to Mr. Hodges.
Imported by Mr. Woodburn.
Mr. Ralph Bernal. Sold 1824, £391, 13s., to Mr. J. Smith, who sold it to the Chevalier Erard.
Chevalier Erard, Château de la Muette, near Paris. Sold 1832, No. 102, 20,000 francs.
Bought of the Prince de Beauveau through Mr. Chaplin, 1848.
Smith, vi. 352, No. 118.
Waagen, *Treasures*, ii. 187. "This charming picture reminds us in composition of Cuyp; it is also painted with greater body than usual, so that the delicacy of this master is combined in some measure with the power of Cuyp."
Kugler, *Handbook*, ii. 501.

119   **3. THE SALUTE.**

Canvas. 26⅞ × 39⅞ in.

On the left a man-of-war, with her sails hanging loose, is firing a salute from her port battery. On the extreme left there is a small vessel with the Dutch arms and colours. In the centre, a six-oared boat full of passengers. On the right, a little farther off, are a frigate at anchor, two coasters, and a small boat. Signed on a buoy on the right with initials.

Collections—Sir Philip Stephens. Sold May 17, 1810, £57, 15s.
            Viscount Ranelagh. Sold June 22, 1821, £53, 0s. 6d., to Mr. Rutley.
            M. Nieuwenhuys. Sold May 11, 1833, £210, to Mr. Hoffman.
            Sir Thomas Baring.
Bought, June 3, 1848, No. 112, £154, 7s.
Smith, vi. 359, No. 137.
Waagen, *Treasures*, ii. 188.
     „   *Handbook*, ii. 466.
Exhibited—British Institution, 1850, No. 137.

GERBRAND VAN DEN EECKHOUT, 1621–1674.

120   **A PHILOSOPHER.**

Panel. 28 × 23½ in.

A lofty vaulted room with a window on the left, near which an old man sits in an arm-chair. He wears a lilac dress, and over it a claret-coloured gown, with collar and facings of brown fur. His feet rest on a wooden stool. In his right hand he holds a pen, while he leans his head against his left. On the table are a number of books, an inkstand, and some papers. On the wall behind are a map and a cupboard, with a bunch of keys in the lock. On a pillow, in the centre, hangs a clock, with a bell and hammer above it. In the foreground stands a globe. In the background, on the right, is a staircase, down which a man is coming, and at its foot a woman-servant sweeping.

Collection—Mr. Thomas Baring.

JAN VAN DER HAGEN, 1635-1679.

121 LANDSCAPE.

Panel. 15½ x 19¾ in.

View at the entrance of a wood. In the centre of the foreground a group of men, one on horseback with a horn slung at his side, the others resting. To the right, two more men advancing with some hounds. On the left, a landscape with a castle in the mid-distance and blue hills. Brilliantly lighted sky with white clouds. The figures probably by Johann Lingelbach.

Collection—Lord Northwick.
Bought, July 26, 1859, No. 68, £69, 6s.
Exhibited—Royal Academy, 1872, No. 187.

BARTHOLOMEW VAN DER HELST, 1613-1670.

122 THE STANDARD-BEARER.

Canvas. 35½ x 26¼ in.

A life-size half-length portrait of the standard-bearer of a guild, his face seen nearly in full. He wears a black dress with a plain white collar and cuffs, and has a broad crimson scarf round his waist, and a sword at his side hanging from a belt thrown over his right shoulder. With his right hand he holds the pole of a standard, his left rests on the hilt of his sword.

Bought from Mr. James Everest, 1857.

JAN VAN DER HEYDE, 1637–1712.

123   VIEW IN A TOWN.

Panel, oak.   19¼ × 22⅞ in.

A canal extends along the whole of the front of the picture; a branch of it receding to the left is crossed by a drawbridge, on which is a woman with a basket on her head. On the bank to the right stands a brick house. Behind it is a lane from which a man is advancing towards the bridge. Beyond the lane is a small red brick house, and adjoining it a church with a classical façade. On the opposite bank on the left are trees, a covered market, and a statue. Close to the bridge are two men leaning on the parapet, and at the foot of some steps is a woman dipping clothes in the water. On the right are two swans; just above them, in the masonry, are the arms of the town. On the left the signature HEYDE. The figures, spiritedly drawn, are by Adrian Van de Velde.

Collections—M. Peter de Smeth van Alphen. Sold August 1, 1810, No. 38.
        2990 florins, to Mr. J. Yver.
        M. Le Brun. Sold 1811, 9051 francs.
        Prince Talleyrand, 1817.
        M. Eynard.
        Prince de Galitzin, Paris. Sold 1825 for 8010 francs, to Mr.
        Broadgeat for Baron Verstolk.
        Verstolk.
Bought in 1846.
Smith, v. 394, No. 84.
Waagen, Treasures, ii. 188.
Exhibited—British Institution, 1850, No. 144.
        Royal Academy, 1872, No. 176.

ARTUS VAN DER NEER, 17th Century.

124

1. DAWN.

Panel. 17¾ × 24⅞ in.

View on a river. On the bank to the left is a village with a church spire, and farther off a windmill. On the opposite bank, in the foreground, two cows close to some pollards. Farther off are trees and houses, and in the mid-distance an extensive building with a large square tower.

Collections—M. Bonn, Amsterdam.
  Verstolk.
Bought in 1846.

125

2. EVENING.

Panel. 17¾ × 24⅞ in.

The companion picture. On the extreme left, in the foreground, is a tree with a cottage behind it. At a gate in front, a woman and a boy are watching a man in red fishing in a boat. Beyond, along the river, are a number of houses and boats. In the centre, in the distance, a lofty church tower. In front, some ducks. Sky covered with clouds, those to the right reddened by the setting sun. Signed on the right with initals.

Collections—M. Bonn, Amsterdam.
  Verstolk.
Bought in 1846.

126

3. MOONLIGHT.

Panel. 14½ × 19¼ in.

In the centre is a river with boats, and buildings on either side. On the right, in front, are posts with nets and a sailing-boat ; farther off a town with a large church with a square tower. On the left, in front, are two boys and a horse ; beyond are houses and windmills. The moon is rising above some clouds in the distance, just over a vessel. Signed on the left with initials.

Collection—Earl of Beverley.
Bought in 1851.

ANTHONY VAN DYCK, 1599–1641.

127   1. ECSTASY OF ST. AUGUSTINE.

Panel, oak.   10¾ × 12 in.

St. Augustine kneeling in an ecstasy, supported by two angels, one of whom is pointing to the Holy Trinity appearing in the clouds above, surrounded by angels holding emblems or playing musical instruments.   The Saint wears a cope ; his mitre and staff lie with some books on the ground before him.   On his right kneels St. Monica with her hands crossed on her breast, and on his left a monk with his hands joined.

A carefully executed sketch in grisaille for the picture (height, 11½ feet, breadth, 6 feet) painted by Vandyck in 1628 for the Church of Saint Augustine at Antwerp, now over the altar in the south chapel.   The design displays much of the influence of Rubens.

A copy of this sketch, formerly in the collections of Mr. Knight and of the Rev. Edward Balme (sold March 1, 1823, No. 52, £6, 6s., to Mr. Seguier), is now in the University Gallery at Oxford.

Collections—Methuen, Catalogue, 1760, p. 39, and 1805, No. 105.
   Sir Thomas Baring.
Bought, June 3, 1848, No. 86, £18, 7s. 6d.
M. Mols, *MS. Notes in the Royal Library at Brussels*, No. 5737, ff. 115v and 117.
Sir Joshua Reynolds, *Works : A Journey to Flanders and Holland*, London, 1809, vol. ii. p. 315.
Smith, iii. 3, No. 5, note.
W. H. Carpenter, *Pictorial Notices of Van Dyke*, London, 1844, pp. 17 and 196.
Waagen, *Treasures*, ii. 182.
Exhibited—Grosvenor Gallery, 1887, No. 156.
Photographed, *Northbrook Gallery*.

The picture is engraved in reverse by Peter de Iode, jun. (10½ × 11½ in.); the engraving dedicated by Van Dyck to his sister Susan, a novice in the Beguinage at Antwerp   Also engraved by Van den Enden (19½ × 11½ in.).

128   2. THE GUITAR-PLAYER.

Canvas.   60¾ × 43 in.

A full-length portrait of a gentleman, small life-size, with long
dark hair, sitting in a chair, turned slightly to the left, with his feet
crossed, playing a ten-stringed lute.   He wears a black figured silk
dress with slashed sleeves, a plain broad white collar and cuffs, and
large buff boots ; his cloak is thrown across his lap.   Dark background.
The figure has more natural, and less artificial, refinement than
usual in Van Dyck.   The treatment is very masterly, the colours very
harmonious, but unusually broken, for Van Dyck.   Probably painted
shortly after his return from Italy to Antwerp.

Collections—M. de Montmartel, Paris, No. 23, 1772.
            Marquis de Brunoy, Paris. Sold December 2, 1776, 6000 francs.
            M. Le Brun, Paris, January 19, 1778.
            M. Poullain, Paris. Sold March 15, 1780, No. 46, 2406 francs.
            M. De Cournont.
            M. le Chevalier Lambert. Sold March 27, 1787, No. 62, 1800
                francs.
            Prince Lucien Bonaparte, 1815, No. 157. Sold 1816, No. 43 (£64).
            Mr. Stanley.
Bought from Mr. Smith, 1853.
Smith, iii. 84, No. 281.
Waagen, *Galleries*, 98.   "In conception and colouring this picture is as
original as it is attractive."
Exhibited—Royal Academy, 8170, No. 38.
            Grosvenor Gallery, 1887, No. 5.

Engraved by Petrini (8¼ × 6¼ in.), in the gallery of Prince Lucien Bonaparte. In
reverse by Brichet, in the Poulain Gallery, Paris, 1731, after a drawing by Moitte
(6 × 4¼ in.).

129   3. EARL OF NEWPORT.

Canvas, 84 × 51 in.

Full length, life size, standing with his head turned three-quarters to the right. He has dark wavy hair, worn low on the forehead, and falling to just below the neck behind; dark brown eyes, a long nose, small moustachio, and a slight imperial. He is dressed in a long buff jacket with slashed sleeves, and loose breeches to match, the whole dress trimmed with silver lace, a steel cuirass with a sash, lace collar and cuffs, and long yellow boots with spurs. His left hand, in a loose white glove, rests on his hip above the hilt of his rapier, and in his right he holds a staff. In the background are some tents, and two men in armour are indistinctly seen to the right. On the left stands a table with a red cloth and some armour upon it. Underneath, in the foreground, are some large dock-leaves.

There is a picture of this nobleman at Petworth (Catalogue, No. 300), painted with Lord Goring and his son; and another, a small full length, belonging to the Duke of Hamilton, was exhibited in the Grosvenor Gallery, 1887 (No. 60).

The head is engraved by Hollar, Droeshout, and Richardson.

Collection—The Earl of Portarlington. Acquired by the Earl of Northbrook by exchange, 1881.

Exhibited—Royal Academy, 1878, No. 147.
            Grosvenor Gallery, 1887, No. 15.

Photographed, *Northbrook Gallery.*

Mountjoy Blount, Earl of Newport, was a natural son of Charles Blount, Earl of Devonshire (Lord Deputy and Lieutenant of Ireland), by Penelope Devereux, sister of Robert, Earl of Essex, and wife of Lord Rich, afterwards Earl of Warwick. The Earl of Devonshire, who died in 1606 without lawful issue, left his estates to Mountjoy Blount, who was created by James I. Lord Mountjoye of Mountjoy Fort in the north of Ireland, and

(90)

VAN DYCK.

by Charles I. Baron Mountjoye of Thurveston in the county of Derby in 1627, and Earl of Newport in the Isle of Wight in 1628.

He commanded 600 horse at the siege of Rhé in 1628, where he was taken prisoner. In 1629 he was fined £3000 for so-called "forest encroachments." In 1630 he was made Warden of Hyde Park on the recommendation of his half-brother, Henry Earl of Holland. In 1635 he was Master of the Ordnance. He was one of the twenty-two peers who sided with the majority of the House of Commons in 1641 against the appointment of Sir Thomas Lunsford as Lieutenant of the Tower in place of Sir William Balfour, "the tried friend of the Parliament." When the House addressed the King to remove Lunsford, Lord Newport was requested to take charge of the place "for the present;" but the King suddenly dismissed him from his post on a charge of disloyal speaking and plotting, which he vehemently denied in a personal altercation with the King. This was on the afternoon of Friday, the 24th of December 1641. On Wednesday the 29th the King informed the House of Lords that he had never believed the charge against the Earl, and desired it to be withdrawn. Oliver Cromwell, then M.P. for Cambridge, led the House in an animated debate on the Earl's dismissal.

Lord Newport joined the King at York in 1642, and signed the Declaration of Peers and Councillors in June of that year. He served on the Royalist side in the Civil War as Lieutenant-General to the Earl of Newcastle in Yorkshire in 1642, and afterwards at Dartmouth, when that place was taken by Fairfax in 1646.

He married in 1627 Anne, daughter of John Boteler or Butler, of Woodhall, Herts, who was created in 1625 Lord Butler of Brantfield. He died February 12, 1665, and was buried in Christ Church Cathedral, Oxford. He left three sons, George, Charles, and Henry, who succeeded in turn to the Earldom, which became extinct on the death of Henry without issue in 1681.

Thomas Milles, *The Catalogue of Honor*. London, William Jaggard, 1610, p. 493.

Dugdale, *Baronage*.

John Forster, *Arrest of the Five Members by Charles the First*. London, J. Murray, 1860, pp. 36–39 and 82.

C. Markham, *Life of Lord Fairfax*. London, Macmillan, 1870, pp. 76, 260.

Clarendon, *Rebellion*. Oxford, 8vo, 1819, i. 579.

130 4. QUEEN HENRIETTA MARIA, SIR JEFFREY
HUDSON, AND A MONKEY.

Canvas. 85¼ × 52 in.

Full-length figures, standing, life size. The Queen stands upon
a step, with her head slightly turned to the left. She has brown
curling hair, with one ringlet falling on her shoulder, oval face, and
brown eyes. She is dressed in a large black felt hat with a white
plume behind, a blue moirée silk gown trimmed with narrow gold
braid, elbow-sleeves with full lace frilling, a lace collar, and a
kerchief over her shoulders with two pink bows in front. With
her left hand she is touching a stiff fold of her dress, while with
her right she caresses a little brown monkey carried on the shoulder
of Sir Jeffrey Hudson, who has a fair, boyish face, and is dressed in
a long jacket and breeches of crimson velvet, a lace collar, and long
brown boots. In the background to the left there is a stone wall
with an orange tree in a flower-pot upon it, and some trees and
the sky behind. In the centre is a fluted pillar, and to the right
a brilliant orange silk curtain, covering a ledge upon which rests
a crown of gold set with pearls.

A similar picture is in the possession of Earl FitzWilliam at
Wentworth (exhibited British Institution, 1846, No. 187, and Manchester, 1857, No. 108). It was described as "given by King
Charles the First to the great Earl of Strafford. Vandyck received
£40 for it." A copy by Jervas is at Petworth (Catalogue, No. 146).

Collection—The Earl of Portarlington. Acquired by the Earl of Northbrook
by exchange, 1884.
Exhibited—Royal Academy, 1878, No. 166.
          Grosvenor Gallery, 1887, No. 15.
Photographed, Northbrook Gallery.

These two pictures were in the possession of the Newports, Earls
of Bradford of the first creation, and were left in 1762, on the
death of the fifth Earl, to his sister, Diana, widow of Algernon
Coote, sixth Earl of Mountrath. They descended to his son, the
seventh and last Earl of Mountrath, and from him to the first Earl
of Dorchester, of Milton Abbey, where they remained till removed
by the present Earl of Portarlington to Emo Park, Ireland.

131   5. ADAM DE COSTER.

Panel. 10 × 7½ in.

A sketch in grisaille. A similar sketch, but lighter in colour (as are the others in the series for the engravings by P. de Jode published in Dr. Wibiral's " Iconographie d'Antoine Van Dyck "), is in the possession of the Duke of Buccleuch. This sketch is more finished, and may be by another hand.

Adam de Coster of Mechlin, a pupil of Rombouts, painted historical subjects, assemblies, night effects, and portraits. The inscription under the engraving is " Adam de Coster, Pictor noctium, Mechliniensis."

Collection—Mr. Thomas Baring.
Exhibited—Grosvenor Gallery, 1887, No. 145.

----

132 JAN VAN GOYEN, 1596–1656.

VIEW ON A RIVER.

Panel. 25¼ × 37½ in.

In front is a strip of land, on which are six cows, and a woman milking one of them. On the river are three boats with men, and on the farther bank a house with a tower, beyond which, on a headland are trees, a church tower and spire, a building with a tower, and a fortified wall with a windmill. On the farther side, on the extreme right, are some cottages and trees. Cloudy sky.

Signed on a boat close to the centre with initials, and the date 1647.

Collection—Earl of Beverley.
Bought in 1851.

(93)

SAMUEL VAN HOOGSTRAETEN, 1627–1678.

133   PORTRAIT.

Panel.   8½ × 6¾ in.

Portrait of an artillery officer, half-length, turned to the left, his face seen in three-quarters. He has long brown hair, a moustachio and an imperial, and wears a sleeveless buff leather dress, with a strap over the right shoulder, slashed sleeves lined with red, and a large collar bordered with lace. Dark background.

In its original frame, which is ornamented with cannon.

Collections—Sir Thomas Baring. Sold June 3, 1848, No. 64, 68, &c., as by Terburg.
Sir Francis T. Baring (Lord Northbrook).

JAN VAN HUYSUM, 1682–1749.

134   VASE WITH FLOWERS.

Panel.   31¼ × 23½ in.

A nosegay of flowers, comprising tulips, jonquils, roses, &c., in a terra-cotta vase decorated with a cupid in relief. Other flowers are lying on the stone table on which the vase stands. Signed.

Bought from M. Nieuwenhuys, 1867.
Exhibited—Royal Academy, 1872, No. 44.

JAN VAN KESSEL, 1648–1698.

135   LANDSCAPE.

Canvas. 31¾ × 38 in.

In the middle of the foreground there is a dark shallow pool of water, with a man and woman on the road to the right walking towards the front, and several other persons beyond standing talking; the road in the middle distance, lit up by a bright gleam of sunshine, winds round to the right up some rising ground; on it are a number of persons, and along its side several fine trees. On the road in the right foreground are two boys with sticks, also a little dog, and behind them two pieces of felled timber, close to which is a man resting with two boys at his side. On the left are two dogs chasing each other on the road, and in the background a fine clump of trees. Cloudy sky.

This is an excellent work; the trunks of the trees are firmly modelled and the aerial perspective remarkably good. Waagen considers it as in the taste of Ruisdael, but it certainly has an individual character of its own. The general effect is that of a summer evening, and the picture is dark. There is not a public museum in Europe that claims to have a picture by this master, who often imitated Philip De Koninck and Hobbema, though more generally, as here, Ruisdael. The figures are probably by Abraham Stork.

Collection—Mr. Thomas Baring.
Waagen, *Galleries*, 99.
Kugler, *Handbook*, ii. 481.

MICHAEL VAN MUSSCHER, 1645–1705.

136   WILLEM VAN DE VELDE THE YOUNGER.

Panel.   18¼ × 14¼ in.

The artist is sitting in his studio preparing his palette.   On his right stands an easel with a tall landscape on it.   On his left is a box of colours, and on the ground in front lie a book of sketches and some studies of shipping.   Round the room hang several landscapes in black frames; three palettes and three panels lean against the wall to the right; on the cornice of the door stand two Roman busts and a statuette of the Farnese Hercules at Naples.

Signed on the pavement in the right corner: MUSSCHER, Pinxit 165.

Engraved by Charles G. Lewis as the frontispiece to Part 6 of Smith's *Catalogue Raisonné.*

Collections—M. Michael Van Musscher, Amsterdam.   Sold April 12, 1706, No. 11, 100 florins.

A collection, Amsterdam.   Sold January 21, 1733, 80 florins.

M. Jacob De Vos, Amsterdam.   Sold July 2, 1833, 600 florins. Verstolk.

Bought in 1846.

Waagen, *Treasures,* ii. 184.   "There is something very pleasing in the feeling of this picture, which in transparency, chiaroscuro, and careful completion in no way falls short of the excellence of Adrian Ostade, Musscher's master."

Kugler, *Handbook,* ii. 401.

Bürger, 277.   "Le chef-d'œuvre de Van Musscher . . . est le precieuse portrait de Willem Van de Velde occupé à peindre dans son atelier."

Photographed, *Northbrook Gallery.*

Exhibited—Royal Academy, 1880, No. 134.

ADRIAN VAN OSTADE, 1610-1685.

137   1. CARD-PLAYERS.

Panel. 17¼ × 14¾ in.

In the foreground, on the left, two peasants playing cards; a little farther back, a third with a jug in his right and a pipe in his left hand looking on, and a boy caressing a dog; farther back to the right, seven more figures, one standing with his back to the chimney-piece, the others seated smoking and talking. From the rafters are suspended three hams and a flitch of bacon; on the walls are a variety of objects. Behind the card-players is a coloured drawing pinned to the wall. Below, to the right, is the signature and date 1648.

Collections—Mr. Holford,
         Mr. William Buchanan.
Bought from Mr. Buchanan, 1850.
Waagen, *Treasures*, ii. 185. "Deep golden tones and great vigour of chiaroscuro are united in this little *chef d'œuvre* with a solid impasto and careful completion."
Kugler, *Handbook*, ii. 420.
Exhibited—Royal Academy, 1871, No. 223, and 1880, No. 125.

138   2. THE MUSICIAN.

Panel. 12¾ × 10½ in.

A man in a purplish jacket and short cloak is playing a hurdy-gurdy before a cottage; at the door, above which is a sloping roof, stands a peasant in a brown coat and red cap, leaning on the wicket, holding a pipe in his left hand. Behind him are a man and woman, and outside, on the left, a boy with a box under his right arm, and a little girl in a blue jacket, yellow skirt, white head-kerchief and apron. Figures three-quarters length. Signed on the right.

Engraved by Charles G. Lewis, 4¾ × 4 in.
Collections—Admiral Lord Radstock. Sold May 13, 1826, No. 25, £94, 10s.
         Mr. P. Rainier. May 24, 1845, No. 28.
         Sir Thomas Baring.
Bought, June 3, 1848, No. 120, £88, 4s.
Waagen, *Treasures*, ii. 185.

ISAAC VAN OSTADE, 1621-1649.

139   WINTER SCENE.

Canvas.   42 × 57¾ in.

A frozen river enlivened with numerous figures.   On the bank in front, to the right, are two boys, one of whom is putting on his skates, and a dog.   Higher up, an inn, at the door of which a waggon has stopped ; the host and two men are standing by while the horse is feeding.   Below, on the ice, is a white horse fastened to a sledge containing five persons ; beyond, another sledge with a bay horse and two men.   In the middle are a number of people skating and sledging.   On the left a windmill.

Collections—M. Peter De Smeth van Alphen, Amsterdam.   Sold August 1,
      1810, No. 73, 520 florins, to Mr. Coopmans.
         Mr. Bromlgeest.
Bought through Mr. Chaplin, 1850.
Waagen, *Treasures*, ii. 185.   "An admirable work of the best period of the
      master.   In addition to his usual vigour and transparency of
      colour, the aerial perspective is very delicately sustained, while
      the treatment is bold and free."
Kugler, *Handbook*, ii. 423.

PETER VAN SLINGELANDT, 1640-1691.

140   INTERIOR : CANDLELIGHT.

Panel.   8 × 10¼ in.

In the centre a young woman seated, turned to the right, her right arm resting on a cask as with an arch smile she smokes a long clay pipe ; opposite to her, on the right, is seated a man in a red jacket and black hat who is looking into a jug. Behind him stands an old woman holding up her finger at the younger one. The scene is lighted by a candle standing on the cask. On the left, in the front, is a table with some onions, a cabbage, and a brass jug on it, and in the background before a fire are a woman, whose back only is seen, a girl, and a dog. The principal figures are three-quarter-length.

This picture was formerly attributed to Schalcken.

Collections—M. De Julienne, Paris.   Sold March 30, 1767, 2410 francs.
            M. Gaignat, Paris.   Sold December 2, 1768, 1500 francs.
            Duchesse de Berri.
Exhibited at Christie's in 1834, and sold for £280 to Mr. George Stone.
Bought from M. Nieuwenhuys, 1840.
Smith, iv. 287, No. 98, and ix. 28, No. 13 (under Schalcken).
Waagen, *Treasures*, ii. 184.   "The painter has surpassed himself here, and approaches his master, Gerard Dou, not only in precision of execution, but in truth and softness."

DOMENICUS VAN TOL, 17th Century.

141   GIRL WITH A PINK.

Panel, oak, rounded top. 12½ × 7⅜ in.

A girl in a drab jacket with green sleeves leans on the sill of an arch, holding in her hand one of the sprays of a pink, which grows in a flower-pot to the right. Above hangs a bird-cage. Inside the arch is a bluish-green curtain ; a lamp hangs behind. This picture is a copy of one by Gerard Dou, formerly in the collections of the Duc de Berri and Lord Ashburton, which was destroyed by fire.* Van Tol in the face of the girl has shown himself nearly equal to his master.

Collections—Mr. G. Muller, Amsterdam. Sold April 2, 1827, No. 70, 1700 florins, to Mr. Brondgeest.

    Verstolk.

Bought in 1846.

Waagen, *Treasures*, ii. 184.

HENDRIK VAN VLIET, 1605–1671.

142   NIEUW KERK AT DELFT.

Canvas. 40¼ × 33½ in.

View taken from the north transept. A man and woman with a dog are standing at the iron railings looking at the bronze statue of William I., Prince of Orange, placed at the head of his tomb in the choir. Farther off are two men and a woman. On the left are two men in conversation, one kneeling, the other standing, and a man and boy with a dog.

Collections—M. William Van Wouw, Amsterdam. Sold May 29, 1764, 71 florins.

    M. B. Ocke, Leiden. April 21, 1817, No. 138.

    Verstolk.

Bought in 1846.

Waagen, *Treasures*, ii. 188.

* Engraved in reverse by Anthony de Marcenay de Ghuy, 1766, as "La Fleuriste" (11 × 8¼ in.). A replica in Lord Northwick's collection was put up at Christie's, May 24, 1838, and bought in at £147.

ABRAHAM VERBOOM, 1610–1663 (?).

143   HILLY LANDSCAPE.

Canvas. $31\frac{1}{2} \times 38\frac{3}{4}$ in.

View of the side of a hill sloping down from left to right, with high trees and a stream, where a man in a blue jacket is spearing a fish. On the right a man and a woman are driving cattle and sheep up a road. A view over an undulating country in the distance. The figures are by Adrian Van de Velde. This picture is set down in some of the Verstolk lists as by Van der Asch.

Collections—M. Héris, Brussels.
         Lucien Buonaparte.
         Verstolk.
Bought in 1846.
Engraved by Parbone, Lucien Buonaparte's Catalogue, No. 31.
Waagen, *Treasures*, ii. 187.
Kugler, *Handbook*, ii. 480. "The best picture by him in England I know."

JAN BAPTIST WEENIX, 1621–1660.

144   1. GAME.

Canvas. $29\frac{1}{2} \times 24$ in.

To the branch of a tree are hung a net, a partridge and a pheasant, a horn and a green hunting-pouch. On the ground in front are two small dead birds. On the right a landscape with trees. Cloudy evening sky.

Collection—Mr. Thomas Baring.

145   2. GAME.

Canvas. 70½ × 65¾ in.

In the foreground to the right, on and round a fragment of antique sculpture, are hung a hare, a rabbit, and a horn. Nearer the front are a cock-pheasant, a brace of partridges, a hoopoe, and other dead birds, and on the extreme right a gun, a pouch, and some plants in flower. On the left a large dog lies with its fore-paws on a wild duck. In the air is a pigeon flying towards another perched at the top of the sculpture. On the left a landscape, with a village in the distance, and a boar-hunt in the mid-distance.

Collections—M. Brentano. Sold May 13, 1822, No. 306, to M. Nieuwenhuys.
         Lord Charles Townshend. Sold June 30, 1849, £173. 5s., to M.
         Nieuwenhuys.
Bought from M. Nieuwenhuys, 1850.
Nieuwenhuys, *Review*, 270.

PHILIP WOUWERMANS, 1619–1668.

146   1. THE SPORTSMAN.

Panel. 12 × 10¼ in.

On the left an old tree with scanty foliage; a peasant advancing to the front has stopped before it, doffing his cap, to speak to a young sportsman in scarlet with a feather in his hat, mounted on a grey horse. Between them a hound. In the distance, on rising ground, are cattle, and still farther off a mountain. Blue sky with clouds, and a couple of birds on the wing. Signed to the right with initials, and the date 1649.

Broadly painted in deep colours in the master's earlier manner.

Collection—Earl of Beverley.
Bought in 1851.
Smith, ix. 196, No. 146.

147   2. THE HORSE-FAIR.

Panel.   20¼ × 18 in.

An inn on the right, at the side of which is an almost leafless tree, and beyond, two tents. The foreground on this side is crowded with figures. The principal group consists of a man on a white horse, one of whose forefeet a groom in a red coat is lifting up, while two gentlemen standing at its head are talking about it Before the inn-door are a lady and gentleman on horseback ; the hostess is handing the latter a glass of liquor. On the extreme right are some men at a table drinking and gambling. To the left are two gentlemen looking at a horse, which is being shown off to them. In the foreground are some beggars. A coach and six is driving up from the village in the distance, where are some tents, cottages, and trees, and behind them a church steeple. Signed on the left with initials.

Engraved by J. Moyreau, 1737.   In the Choiseul Gallery.
Collections—M. le Chevalier Hallé, 1737.
              Duc de Choiseul, Paris. Sold April 6, 1772, No. 57, with it-
              fellow, 20,000 francs.
              Marquis de Voyer d'Argenson.
              Prince de Conti, Paris. Sold April 8, 1777, No. 342, with it-
              fellow, 19,800 francs.
              M. Durney, Paris. Sold June 21, 1797, 4601 francs.
              M. Joseph Augustine Brentano, Amsterdam. Sold May 13, 1822
              No. 372, 4010 florins, to M. Broadgeest.
              Verstolk.
Bought in 1846.
Smith, i. 232, No. 106.
Waagen, *Treasures*, ii. 186. "A rich picture in his second manner, and of delicate quality."
Exhibited—British Institution, 1850, No. 6.

JAN WYNANTS, c. 1620–1679.

148   LANDSCAPE.

16 × 18¾ in.

On the right, in the foreground, is a pool of water, with a man sitting on the farther bank fishing ; another, by his side, is talking to him. On the left, some rising ground, trees, and a thatched cottage, up to which a sandy road leads from the foreground, near which there lie some trunks of trees. In the mid-distance, a grove of trees and a village with a church. Beyond are hills and a distant tower. Blue sky with some clouds to the right.

A very good early picture. Signed to the left of centre with the date 1643.

Bought of Mr. Smith, 1847.
Waagen, *Treasures*, ii. 187.
Exhibited—Royal Academy, 1871, No. 221.

149   2. LANDSCAPE AND CATTLE.

Canvas. 13¼ × 16½ in.

On the left, some rising ground with trees. In the foreground, a fallen tree, near which are a goat and a sheep, and above them a man in a red jacket. On the right, two cows and some sheep, and a road, with some people advancing. In the distance, a country-house and water with a boat on it, and farther off a town. Warm sky with a few clouds. Signed on the left with the date 1670.

Collection—Sir Thomas Baring.
Bought, June 3, 1848, No. 134, £110, 5s.
Waagen, *Treasures*, ii. 187.

ITALIAN SCHOOL.

ANTONELLO DA MESSINA, c. 1412-1493.

150   1. SAINT JEROME IN HIS STUDY.

Panel, poplar. 18⅛ × 14⅛ in.

Through a depressed archway, on the step of which are a quail, a peacock, and a brass basin, is seen the interior of a lofty vaulted cruciform building of stone. The central bay, or transept, of this interior is occupied by a wooden dais or platform reached by a narrow flight of three steps. Here is seated the Saint, in a deep chair with a rounded open-work back, at a table ending in a reading-desk. He wears a large red skull-cap, and a long, tight-sleeved linen rochet, and over it the usual cardinal's red mantle— *cappa magna*; the hood, falling over his shoulders, is lined with brown fur. He is about to turn over the leaf of a folio manu-script lying open on the desk before him. On the table are an inkstand with a pen and two books; on the shelves at the back of both table and platform are more books, some open, others closed, a bottle and a pot of blue and white ware, several little boxes, and a basket. Above the shelves facing the Saint is a crucifix; and behind his chair, at the extreme right of the platform, a wooden coffer with his cardinal's hat lying on it. Attached to the side of the table is a sheet of paper which appears to bear a signature beneath three lines of writing; but, when examined with a magnifying glass, this proves to be an illusion. On the edge of the platform are a white cat, a pot of pinks, and a pot with a small orange-tree. On a wooden peg at the side of the shelves hang a fringed towel and a leather pencase; at the foot of the steps lie a pair of wooden shoes. High above the Saint's head is an unglazed Gothic window divided by a slender column into two trefoil-headed lights beneath a round arch. On the sill of this and two similar windows over the side bays sit some small birds, while others are flying round. Under the window, on the right, is a vaulted hall divided by a row of slender columns supporting round arches. Two rectangular windows at the further end give a view of a landscape with distant hills. In the nearer aisle is seen a lion approaching, with a fore-paw lifted. On the left is a room with a window looking out on a landscape crossed by a stream. In a garden on the near side of the stream is a lady in black walking with a white dog; there is a boat with two men in white rowing on the water, and on the further bank a man in red. Beyond are fields and two cross-roads running past a castle with two towers and a church surrounded by walls, opposite to which is another garden enclosed by a stone wall. On the road are two horsemen, mounted, one on a black, the other on a white horse. In the distance, some hills.

This is a wonderful piece of painting; the outline is firm, the colouring rich and admirably blended, with great breadth of light and shade. Though the details are represented with extraordinary minuteness, they do not obtrude themselves on the attention, which is at once arrested by the figure of the Saint. The expression of concentrated thought in his face is a real masterpiece, while the solemn stillness of the shadowed interior, so thoroughly in keeping with the subject, is ably relieved by the glimpses of animated life in the joyous sunlight without.

Vasari [*] speaks of a picture representing Saint Jerome, painted by Jan van Eyck, that belonged to Lorenzo de Medici. It is just possible that this may be the picture above described.

Dr. Waagen, who saw the picture in 1835 at Stratton (it was then ascribed to Albert Durer), considered it to be by Van Eyck, and discovered an ancient description of it, which he gives as follows in a note to his work:—

" In the notices relative to the arts by an anonymous writer of
the first half of the sixteenth century, which Morelli published at
Bassano in the year 1800,* there is at page 74 the following account
of the little picture, then (1529) in the possession of Antonio
Pasqualino at Venice :—

" ' El quadretto del S. Jeronimo, che nel studio legge in abito
Cardinalesco, alcuni credono che el sii stato de mano de Antonello
da Messina : ma li più, e più verisimilmente l'attribuiscono a Gianes
(i.e., John van Eyck), ovvero al Memelin (Hans Memlinc) pittor
antico Ponentino : è cussi mostra quella manierà, benchè il volto è
finito alla Italiana ; sicchè pare de man de Jacometto. Li edificii
sono alla Ponentina, el paesetto è naturale, minuto, e finito, e si
vide oltra una finestra, e oltra la porta del studio, e pur fugge ;
e tutta l'opera per sottilità, colori, disegno, forza, e rilevo è perfetta.
Ivi sono ritratti uno pavone, un colorno, e un bacil de barbiero
espressamente. Nel scabello vi è finta una letterina attaccata
aperta, che pare contener el nome del maestro ; e nondimeno, se si
riguarda sottilmente appresso, non contiene lettera alcuna, ma è
tutta finta. Altri credono che la figura sii stata rifatta da Jacometto Veneziano.' "

Of the four masters to whom this painting was at that time
ascribed, we can with absolute certainty reject the claims of two,
namely, Van Eyck and Memlinc. As the panel is of poplar-wood,
it was most probably painted in Italy. The painter called Jacometto
by the anonymous writer above quoted is certainly the same person
as Jacopo de' Barbari, the Venetian painter and engraver, called by
the Germans Jacop Walch, and better known as the master of the
Caduceus (c. 1450—c. 1514), none of whose authentic works have
come under our observation.

Though the modelling of the birds and animals, and the technical
execution, differ considerably—being more Bellinesque—from the
panel in the Museum at Antwerp, we think that this little gem may
with probability be attributed to Antonello, whose manner, at suc-
cessive periods of his life, differed widely : for who would attribute
the Salvator Mundi of the National Gallery, the Calvary of the

* Known as the " Anonimo di Morelli."

ITALIAN.

Antwerp Museum, and the well-known portrait from the Pourtales Gallery in the Louvre, to the same hand, were it not for the documentary evidence that establishes their common origin.[*]

Collections—Sir Thomas Baring. Sold June 3, 1848, No. 66, to Mr. William
        Coningham, £130, 13s.
        Mr. Coningham.
Bought June 9, 1849, No. 29, £162, 15s.
Waagen, *Art and Artists*, iii. 42.
    „   *Treasures*, ii. 182.
Crowe and Cavalcaselle, ii. 98, 99.
Charles Ephrussi, *Jacopo de Barbari: Notes et Documents Nouveaux*, in the
" Gazette des Beaux-Arts," 2ᵉ Période, tom. xiii., Paris, 1876, p. 365.
W. Schmidt, *Antonello di Messina*, in the "Allgemeines Künstler-Lexikon,"
vol. ii., Leipzig, 1878, p. 126, col. 2.
Exhibited—British Institution, 1848, No. 66.
        Royal Academy, 1871, No. 191.

NOTE BY SIR J. C. ROBINSON.

There are indications that at some period of his career (doubtless before he settled at Venice) Antonello di Messina visited and probably resided for some time in Spain, presumably in that part of the Peninsula then under the sway of his sovereign, Alfonzo King of Aragon Naples and Sicily. That the present picture is the work of Antonello, and that this residence in Spain is a fact, is indirectly evidenced in it.

In Catalonia, Aragon, and the district of Valencia, during the fourteenth and fifteenth centuries, a peculiar local style of domestic architecture, characterised by great uniformity in main features and details, widely prevailed. The interior represented in this picture is, with some inessential modifications to meet pictorial exigencies, a literal representation of the *patio*, or central apartment of a Valencian or Catalonian house, such as there are many still extant, little if at all changed, in the cities of Valencia and Barcelona. The two-light window, divided by a slender central shaft, is known in Spain as the *ajimez* window. This type is quite peculiar to the districts of Spain in question, where hundreds of examples are still to be seen. There cannot be a doubt, in short, that the interior here depicted with so much verisimilitude, was carefully copied from an existing building, probably the house of one of the rich merchants of Valencia.

                                                                J. C. ROBINSON.

---

[*] The description of this picture is by Mr. Weale.

FRA BARTOLOMMEO (BACCIO DELLA PORTA),
(ASCRIBED TO), 1469–1517.

151 I. HOLY FAMILY.

Panel. 41⅞ × 30½ in.

The Virgin seated, turned to the left, holds the infant Christ on her knees. He raises his right hand, looking towards the infant St. John, who stands to the left, with the hand of a person not in the picture resting on his shoulder. Above is a balustrade with the sketch of a head, probably of Joseph. This is an unfinished work of special interest. It has been ascribed to Raphael * and Fra Bartolommeo. Crowe and Cavalcaselle consider it to be later than Fra Bartolommeo, and ascribe it to Raphael del Colle. It appears to bear so great a similarity to the Holy Family by Pierino del Vaga in this collection, No. 218, that it may with greater probability be ascribed to that master.

Collections—Gregori, Fuligno.
　　　　　Sir Augustus Foster, 1840.
Bought 1855.
Waagen, *Galleries*, 93. "The two children alone are carried out with careful modelling in colour, otherwise the ground is only covered with a thin surface of brown lake, with the outlines drawn in with the brush in dark brown colour. In the Virgin are seen indications of grey shadows. The background is black. In a technical point of view this picture is very interesting."
Crowe and Cavalcaselle, iii. 475.
Exhibited—Royal Academy, 1871.

---

* Some interesting documents regarding this picture, and the reasons for attributing it to Raphael, are in my possession.—*N.*

152   2. HOLY FAMILY.

Panel. 42 × 32 in.

Full length figures, half life-size. The Virgin is seated, with her head turned to the left, dressed in crimson with a mantle. She holds the child in her lap. He is blessing the infant St. John, who kneels to the left with a cross over his right shoulder. The head of Joseph is seen behind to the right. Landscape background to the left, with a town and hills.

Collection—Hamilton Palace.
Bought by the Earl of Northbrook, 1882, No. 711, £225.
Photographed, *Northbrook Gallery.*

IL BASSANO (GIACOMO DA PONTE), 1510–1592.

153   LANDSCAPE AND CATTLE.

Canvas. 59 × 49½ in.

A woman is sitting in the foreground ; a boy stands on her right looking at a dog. On the left is a woman kneeling ; opposite her a girl watering some sheep. Behind are two cows and a man. Bushes and blue mountains in the background.

Collections—Sir Thomas Baring. Sold to Mr. Coningham, 1843.
          Mr. Coningham.
Bought June 9, 1849, No. 47, £210.
Waagen, *Art and Artists,* iii. 36.
          Galleries, 96.
Exhibited—British Institution, 1839, No. 13.

GIOVANNI BELLINI (ASCRIBED TO), 1426–1516.

154   VIRGIN AND CHILD.

Panel. 37 × 29 in.

The Virgin, three-quarters length, half life-size, is seated, dressed in a blue mantle with gold border lined with dark brown a light pink dress and white head-dress. The infant Christ sits on her right knee. Behind, to the left, is a green curtain with an embroidered border. To the right a hilly landscape. Blue sky with evening clouds. Below, in the foreground, is the top of a balustrade with the inscription :—

IOANNES·BELLINVS·

This picture is a replica of the central group of a picture in the sacristy of the church "del Redentore" at Venice, representing the Virgin and Child with St. Francis and St. Jerome on either side. Both pictures are traditionally ascribed to Giovanni Bellini, but were more probably painted by Vicenzio di Bragio, called Catena, of Treviso, who died at Venice in 1531. Catena's authorship of the Venice picture was first recognised by the Senatore Giovanni Morelli, a distinguished connoisseur. The differences between the two pictures are few and of little importance. In the Venice picture the folds of the draperies are rather more complicated and harder in outline, the curtain is red, and the landscape in the background is wanting.*

---

* Other genuine works by Catena are St. Jerome (No. 694), and the Warrior adoring the Infant Christ (No. 234), in the National Gallery, catalogued as "ascribed to Giovanni Bellini and his school." The same peculiarities of style will be recognised as in the picture here described. The somewhat less severe conception is probably due to the works in the National Gallery having been painted later.

(111)

Dr. Gustavo Frissoni of Milan says in a letter addressed to Dr. Richter, October 28, 1878, in reference to this picture:—"Il suo vero autore, che non è certamente Bellini (del cui nome si è tanto abusato) non vuol essere altro che il Trevisano Vicenzio Catena di cui trovammo un quadro segnato, di maniera assolutamente simile, nella galleria di Padova."

Collections—A Gallery in Venice.
   Le Brun.
   Sir Thomas Baring. Sold to Mr. Holford, 1843.
   Mr. Coningham.
Bought June 9, 1849, No. 47, £183, 15s.
Le Brun, i. 29. Engraved, No. 15.
Waagen, *Art and Artists*, iii. 35.
Crowe and Cavalcaselle, i. 187, who attribute the Venice picture to Rondolo, "whose replica of it is to be found under its proper name in the Casa Alvise Mocenigo in Venice."

IL BRONZINO (ANGIOLO ALLORI), 1502–1571.

155   PORTRAIT.

Panel. 25 × 19 in.

A young man, life-size, half length, head turned to the right; black dress and cap. He wears a rich gold chain round his neck, with a medallion of St. Michael with the sword and scales. A green curtain in the background.

This is probably one of the artist's earliest works painted before 1530. The influence of Pontormo is seen in the roundness of the modelling and the brownish tones of the flesh-tints.

Bought from Mr. Graves, 1858.

GIULIANO BUGIARDINI, 1475-1554.

156   ST. JOHN THE BAPTIST.

> Panel.   22¾ × 16 in.   The panel is bordered by a Renaissance
> ornament on blue ground.

St. John sits in the centre, turned to the left, with a skin round
his loins.   His red mantle lies on the ground.   In his left hand is
a cross with a small banner inscribed E.A.D.F.Q.P.*   He is drinking out of a wooden bowl which he holds with his right hand.
Opposite him, to the left, are some rocks with bushes, and a fountain.   Trees and a house in the distance to the right.

This picture closely resembles one signed by Bugiardini in the
Academia delle Belle Arti in Bologna (No. 25).   The idea of the
figure seems to have been taken from the statue of St. John,
ascribed to Michael Angelo, in the Palazzo Gualandi at Pisa.

Collections—Marchese Guadagni, Florence.
  Mr. Samuel Woodburn.   Sold June 24, 1853, No. 67, £141, 15s.
    (as by Raphael), to Mr. Cole.
Bought of Mr. Morris Moore, 1855.
Waagen, *Galleries*, 95, ascribes this picture to Marco Palmezzano da Forli.
Crowe and Cavalcaselle, iii. 98.
Photographed, *Northbrook Gallery*.

---

* Ecce agnus Dei ecce qui [tollit] peccata [mundi].—St. John i. 29.

CANALETTO (ANTONIO CANAL), 1697–1748.

157   THE RIALTO AT VENICE.

Canvas. 66½ × 44 in.

In the foreground, to the left, is the Canale Grande, with four gondolas and many figures.   To the right, the façade of a church with four columns.   There are statues of two lions on the corners of the quay.   In the background are palaces and the bridge of the Rialto.

Dr. Waagen was inclined to attribute this picture to Canaletto's nephew, Bernando Bellotto (1725–1780), but there is no sufficient reason to doubt its authenticity.   The Ponte di Rialto (rivo alto) was built by Antonio da Ponte between the years 1588 and 1591.   The buildings in the foreground are introduced from elsewhere.

Collection—Sir Thomas Baring.
Waagen, *Treasures*, ii. 179.

GIROLAMO DA CARPI* (ASCRIBED TO), 1501-1568.

158   HOLY FAMILY AND TWO ANGELS.

Panel.   11¼ × 9¾ in.

The Virgin, turned to the right, holds the infant with her right
arm, and with her left hand lifts a white cloth from a basket lying
on the ground before her.   Joseph kneels beside her.   To the left,
two angels stand behind looking down at the infant, one holding
the chalice, the other the reed with the sponge.   In the background,
blue mountains and a lake with houses on the shore.

Girolamo da Carpi was a scholar of Garofalo, but he painted also
in the manner of Michael Angelo and of other artists.   Pictures very
different in their style may therefore correctly be attributed to him.
It is nevertheless very improbable that he, or any of his contemporaries, was the author of this picture, which both in its conception
and execution appears to belong to the middle Italian school of the
first part of the seventeenth century.   The figures, especially the
angels, are conceived after the ideals of the Carracci.   The picture
is very carefully executed, and in a good state of preservation.

Collection—Sir Thomas Baring.
Waagen, *Treasures*, ii. 178.

---

* According to Vasari, he was born at Ferrara in 1501; according to Superbi,
in 1488.

AGOSTINO CARRACCI, 1558–1601.

159   THE APOSTLES ROUND THE TOMB OF
THE VIRGIN.

Canvas.   35 × 75½ in.

The Apostles are assembled round a sarcophagus which stands in
the centre, some looking down into it, others up to heaven.   St.
Peter kneels to the left, St. John to the right.   A river is seen
in the middle distance ; an extensive landscape—with trees, hills,
and the pyramid of Caius Cestius—in the background.   Cloudy
evening sky.

In this large composition the founder of the Eclectic School has
taken Florentine artists as his model.   The idealised landscape is
an early specimen of the so-called "classical landscapes" in which
Gaspar Poussin and Claude afterwards excelled.

Collections—Cardinal Mellini, Rome.
Sir Thomas Baring.
Waagen, *Treasures*, ii. 179.

ANNIBALE CARRACCI, 1560-1609.

160   1. VIRGIN AND CHILD WITH ST. FRANCIS.

Panel.   17½ × 14¼ in.

The Virgin sits to the left with a book in her right hand ; with her left she supports the infant Christ, dressed in a white tunic, on her knees.   He bends to the right, blessing St. Francis, who kneels in adoration with his hands crossed on his breast.   An angel from behind presents him.   To the right, in the middle distance, is Joseph with the ass.   In the background two arches of a colonnade, through which a distant landscape is seen.

The composition of this picture was apparently influenced by Correggio's Madonna di San Girolamo at Parma, the attitude of St. Francis being like that of the charming figure of Mary Magdalen in that picture.

This picture is a replica of one at Bridgewater House (No. 81), which was bought by the Duke of Bridgewater for £500 from the Orleans Gallery.   It is engraved by A. Romanet in the "Gallerie du Palais Royal," and was reckoned one of Annibale Carracci's best works.   It has been erroneously called the Vision of St. Francis, for no apparition of the Madonna to the Saint is recorded among his legends, or represented among the twenty-eight scenes of his life painted by Giotto in the Church of St. Francis at Assisi.

Collection—Sir Thomas Baring.
Waagen, *Treasures*, ii. 179.
Exhibited—British Institution, 1819, No. 148, and 1840, No. 3.

161   2. LANDSCAPE.

Canvas.   14⅞ × 19¾ in.

To the left a pool with steep banks covered with bushes.   In the foreground, to the right, trees, under which a nymph reclines attended by a satyr; clothes and hunting gear on the left, and two dogs in the centre.   In the middle distance, satyrs and nymphs. Blue background.

Collection—Sir Thomas Baring.
Waagen, *Art and Artists*, iii. 37.
Exhibited—British Institution, 1816, No. 42.
                    Royal Academy, 1872, No. 204.

ITALIAN.

LUDOVICO CARRACCI, 1555–1619.

162   1. ENTOMBMENT.

Panel. 16 × 12 in.

The body of Christ, partly covered by a white cloth, is being placed into the tomb by two men. In the foreground, to the left, Mary Magdalen kneels, contemplating the crown of thorns which she holds in her hands. Behind her stands the Virgin in a blue mantle, her hands clasped in agony. Near her, a woman holding a torch. In the background to the left a rock, to the right a blue distance with a town and the Calvary. Evening sky.

This picture is a very characteristic one. The drawing is accurate, the composition dramatically conceived in accordance with the principles of the Roman school, while in the costumes and the type of the figures in the foreground Titian has been apparently taken as a model. The attitude of Christ bears a striking resemblance to Michael Angelo's statue of the Pietà at Rome.

Collections—Le Brun.
          Sir Thomas Baring.
Le Brun, i. 94. Engraved No. 72.
Waagen, *Treasures*, ii. 179.
Exhibited—British Institution, 1819, No. 148.

163

2. PIETA.

Panel. $22\frac{1}{2}$ × 17 in.

The Virgin, in a blue dress, is seated leaning against the tomb, with the body of Christ, whose head she supports with her right hand, on her knees. To the right are two cherubs; one holds Christ's right hand, the other holds his hands over the crown of thorns. There is a brook in the foreground, a dark hill in the background, with a piece of blue sky to the left.

This composition was a favourite one of Ludovico Carracci and his school. The accurate design, the firmness of modelling, and the cool tone of the colouring, prove this picture to be a genuine work. It was formerly ascribed to Annibale Carracci.

There is a much larger representation of the same subject without the cherubs, erroneously ascribed to Annibale, in the Doria Palace Rome (III. Braccio, No. 18). In the Dulwich Gallery there is a similar picture (No. 311, canvas, $14\frac{1}{2}$ × $18\frac{3}{4}$) with slight variations, one cherub being occupied with the nails instead of the crown of thorns. It was also erroneously ascribed to Annibale.

Bought from Mr. J. Smith, 1856.
Exhibited—Royal Academy, 1871, No. 194.

164

3. BATHSHEBA.

Panel, transferred to canvas. $38\frac{1}{2}$ × $34\frac{3}{4}$ in.

Bathsheba is sitting in the foreground, near the edge of a fountain, combing her hair. A maid stands behind holding a white cloth, another kneels with a jug; behind her is a boy. To the right is a statuette of a Cupid, with a palace in the background. Figures half-life size.

The types and attitudes are imitated from Correggio.

Collections—Le Brun.
          Sir Thomas Baring.
Le Brun, i. 94. Engraved No. 73.
Waagen, Art and Artists, iii. 37.
Exhibited—British Institution, 1840, No. 19.

165   4. ADORATION OF THE SHEPHERDS.

Copper.   22½ × 30 in.

The Virgin sits in the centre, with the infant in her lap.
Behind her Joseph, and a peasant woman with a basket of eggs.
On the right another woman, kneeling, presents a basket with
doves.   An old man stands before her shading his eyes with his
hand from the light which radiates from the child.   Opposite the
Virgin other peasants kneel; near them are a dog and a sheep.
The scene is under an open cottage with a thatched roof; a boy
with a basket is taking off his hat as he enters from the left,
another boy is looking over a wall behind.   Above is a group of
three winged angels' heads.   The full moon is seen to the left, and
morning breaking to the right.

In this picture the artist very closely follows Correggio's famous
" La Notte " (which was at that time at Reggio), both in the composition of the figures and in the effect of the light.   The same
dog is introduced.   The light from the infant gradually diminishing
is well balanced with the shadows, but does not attain the same
magical brightness as in Correggio's picture.

Collection—Sir Thomas Baring.
Waagen, *Treasures*, ii. 179.
Exhibited—British Institution, 1816, No. 54.

CORREGGIO.

166   5. CHRIST BEARING HIS CROSS, AND
ST. VERONICA.

Canvas. 49 × 38 in.

Figures three-quarters length, life size. To the right, Christ—clad in grey—with a cord round his neck, and wearing the crown of thorns—is sinking exhausted to the ground with his left hand on a stone. The cross is over his right shoulder, and is being supported by St. Veronica, who stands to the left, dressed in crimson, with a brown head-dress. This picture was attributed to Annibale Carracci. It is probably by a scholar of Ludovico's.

Engraved in reverse by F. Poilly, 17 × 14 in.
Collection—Sir Thomas Baring.
Waagen, *Art and Artists*, iii. 37.

CORREGGIO, ANTONIO ALLEGRI (ASCRIBED TO),
1494–1529.

167   TWO HEADS OF ANGELS.

Canvas. 10¼ × 19½ in.

The angel on the right looks over his left shoulder, the other bends to the left. Yellow background. Life size.

These appear to be ancient copies, painted between 1526 and 1530, of two heads of angels represented by Correggio in fresco on the cupola of the Cathedral of Parma. But they do not entirely correspond with any of the angels in those frescoes, though the head to the right is very like that of the angel who sits on the balustrade.

Collection—Sir Thomas Baring.
Waagen, *Treasures*, ii. 178.
Exhibited—British Institution, 1816, No. 41, and 1840, No. 8.

(121)   Q

ITALIAN.

CORREGGIO, SCHOOL OF.

168   VIRGIN AND CHILD WITH ST. CATHARINE
AND ST. CLARA.

Panel.   15⅞ × 14 in.

The Virgin is seated in the centre, in a low red dress and a blue
mantle, holding the infant Christ at her breast.   On the right
St. Clara stands with a monstrance in her right hand and a lily in
her left.   On the left is St. Catharine of Alexandria with a book
and a palm-branch, and the fragment of a wheel at her feet.   A
group of trees behind.

This picture has been ascribed to Francesco Maria Rondani
(1505–1548), but is probably by the hand of Michelangelo Anselmi,
called Michelangelo da Parma and Michelangelo da Siena.   He was
born at Lucca in 1491, and studied at Siena under Sodoma.   He
afterwards settled at Parma, where he fell under the influence of
Correggio.   He was living in 1554, but the exact date of his death
is not known.   A picture by him of the Virgin and Child with St.
John the Baptist and St. Stephen, in the Louvre, corresponds
entirely in style with this picture, which is in a perfect state of
preservation.

Collection—Sir Thomas Baring.
Waagen, *Art and Artists*, iii. 36.

PIETRO BERETTINI DA CORTONA, 1598–1669.

169   1. THE MAGDALEN AND ANGELS.

Canvas.   35 × 36½ in.

Mary Magdalen is seated to the right, with her hands on her bosom. Behind her are two angels, with the emblems of the Passion. Figures small life size. Rocks and a wooded landscape in the background.

This picture is one of his best works on canvas, both for colouring, drawing, and composition.

Collection—Sir Thomas Baring.

170   2. ST. JEROME.

The Saint kneels, holding a crucifix in his left hand, and his right arm extended. A skull and some books lie on a bank before him, and to the right are seen the head and shoulders of the lion. Three angels in the clouds above, and five girls dancing in the middle distance.

Collections—Medici, Palazzo Riccardi Florence.
         Le Brun.
         Sir Thomas Baring.
Le Brun, i. 23.   Engraved No. 11.
Exhibited—British Institution, 1816, No. 72.

171   3. INFANT CHRIST AND ST. JOHN.

Canvas.   9¾ × 11½ in.

Christ, seated on a bank, caresses the cheek of St. John, who
kneels before him to embrace him. To the left there is a lamb.
Landscape background.

Collection—Sir Thomas Baring.
Exhibited—British Institution, 1840, No. 17.

172   4. ADORATION OF THE SHEPHERDS.

Canvas.   38¾ × 53 in.

To the right the Virgin kneels before the cradle in which the
child lies, a glory from him lighting the whole picture. Joseph
stands in the centre. Shepherds are presenting their gifts. Behind
are an ox and an ass, and above the cradle two angel boys holding
a scroll with the inscription : GLORIA IN (excels)IS DEO.

Collections—Le Brun.
         Sir Thomas Baring.
Le Brun, i. 23. Engraved No. 10. "Cette admirable production provient
d'un des palais de Rome."

GIUSEPPE MARIA CRESPI, 1665-1747.

173   SPANISH GIRL.

Panel.   14½ × 10½ in.

Full-length figure of a girl standing with a basket in her right hand, and feeding some poultry with her left. Trees and grey sky in the background.

Collections—De Gagny.
          Duc de Chabot. Sold December 1784, No. 7, 1630 francs, to
          M. Remy.
          Sir Francis Baring.
          Sir Thomas Baring.
Waagen, *Art and Artists*, iii. 30.
    „   *Treasures*, ii. 180.
Exhibited—British Institution, 1810, No. 152, and 1837, No. 82.

CARLO CRIVELLI, 1430?–1495?

1. VIRGIN AND CHILD.

Panel.   14 × 9½ in.

Half-length figure of the Virgin standing behind a balustrade. She wears a dark blue damask mantle richly decorated with gold embroidery and lined with green, a transparent veil, and a white head-dress fastened by a chain of pearls. She tenderly supports the infant Christ, who sits on a violet cushion on the balustrade holding a goldfinch in both hands. The nimbs of the infant Christ and of his mother are gilt and decorated with gems. On the balustrade lies a yellowish satin cloth, on which is affixed a paper with the inscription :—

Behind the Virgin a crimson curtain is suspended by a red cord. A wreath of apples and cucumbers hangs above. On each side of the curtain a landscape is seen with high trees, a castle, and some men, two in Turkish costumes, standing about.

Carlo Crivelli was a scholar of the Vivarini, and worked chiefly at Ascoli and its neighbourhood. He continued to paint in tempera while his contemporaries had adopted the new method of oil-painting, but his thinly-painted pictures still retain their original brightness.

This picture has the special interest of being one of his earliest works, it comes very near to his Virgin and Child in the Picture Gallery of Verona, which is the earliest painted by him. After the year 1490, Crivelli always added to his name the word *Miles* (knight), and in his latest works, *Miles Laureatus*.

Collection—Mr. W. Jones of Clytha.
Bought May 8, 1852, No. 103, £157, 10s.
Waagen, *Galleries*, 95.
Crowe and Cavalcaselle, i. 92.
Exhibited—Royal Academy, 1870, No. 235.
Photographed, *Northbrook Gallery*.

175   2. THE RESURRECTION.

Panel, quatrefoil shaped.   20 × 18 in.

In the centre Christ rises from the tomb, a richly ornamented
sarcophagus, upon the edge of which he places his right foot.   In
his left hand he holds a banner with a red cross on a white field.
His right hand is raised in the act of blessing ; a disk nimbus over
his head.   On each side of the tomb, and in front of it, are three
soldiers lying on the ground asleep ; rocks and a town in the distance.   Part of an altar-piece, probably the centre of a predella.

Bought from Messrs. Colnaghi, 1854.
Waagen, *Galleries*, 95.
Crowe and Cavalcaselle, 192.

176   3. ST. BERNADIN AND ST. CLARE.

Panel.   14 × 17 in.   23 × 9 in., including the frame with
Gothic ornaments.

Whole-length figures, standing.   St. Bernadin, in a grey habit,
holds a red book in his left hand, and an oval plate in his right
with the monogram of Jesus.   On his right
stands St. Clare in a grey habit and black
mantle, with a lily in her left hand.   Yellow
disk-nimbs round the heads.   A balustrade
and a green curtain behind.   Gilt background.

The Franciscan monk Bernadin of Siena
was much venerated in Tuscany as a peniten-
tial preacher.   He died at Aquila in 1444, and
was canonised in 1450.   As his head is decorated by a nimb in this picture, it must have
been painted after 1450.   The cipher on the
oval which he holds in his hand is an abbre-

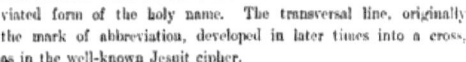

viated form of the holy name.   The transversal line, originally
the mark of abbreviation, developed in later times into a cross,
as in the well-known Jesuit cipher.

Bought from Mr. Bentley, 1856.
Crowe and Cavalcaselle, i. 92.

CARLO DOLCI, 1619–1686.

177   1. CHRIST BEARING HIS CROSS.

Canvas.   21½ × 18 in.

Half length, life size, head turned to the right.   The cross rests on the left shoulder of our Saviour, supported by both his hands. He is dressed in a red tunic and blue mantle.   On his head is the crown of thorns, behind which is a cruciform nimbus of rays.   This picture is a very characteristic and genuine work of the artist.

Collections—Medici, Palazzo Riccardi Florence.
            Le Brun.
            Sir Thomas Baring.
Engraved by C. Heath in Forster's British Gallery.
Le Brun, i. 25.   Engraved No. 14.
Buchanan, ii. 253.
Passavant, i. 281.
Exhibited—British Institution, 1816, No. 114, and 1840, No. 32.

178   2. MATER DOLOROSA.

Canvas.   Oval.   26¼ × 19½ in.

Half length, life size, head turned to the left.   Red dress and blue mantle, the hands folded, the head bent forwards.   A favourite subject of the master.   A replica with some slight variations is in the collection of the Earl of Dudley.

Collections—Chevalier Boucheron.
            Mr. Thomas Hope.
            Sir Thomas Baring.
Waagen, Art and Artists, iii. 38.
     „   Treasures, ii. 176.
Exhibited—British Institution, 1840, No. 27.

DOMENICHINO (DOMENICO ZAMPIERI), 1581-1641.

179   1. INFANT CHRIST WITH THE EMBLEMS
OF THE PASSION.

Panel. 7¼ × 5¾ in.

Full length, about five years old, clad in a blue tunic, sitting
with his right foot on the cross, which lies on the ground. In
his right hand he holds a nail, and by his side is a basket containing a hammer, the crown of thorns, and a cord. Landscape
background.

A replica of this picture, from the Coesvelt and Rogers collections, is in the possession of Baroness Burdett-Coutts. Domenichino and his contemporaries of the Bolognese school were the
earliest of the Italian painters who represented the infant Christ
with the emblems, under the influence of the religious feeling then
prevailing.

Collection—Sir Thomas Baring.
Waagen, *Treasures*, ii. 179.
Exhibited—British Institution, 1841, No. 34.
    Royal Academy, 1871, No. 228.

180   2. LANDSCAPE—RIPOSO.

Canvas. 16 × 18½ in.

In the centre of the foreground, the Virgin reposes on the ground in a red dress, blue mantle, and white head-dress. The infant Christ stands behind her, near them Joseph asleep, and the ass grazing to the right. Other figures and a horse in the middle distance. High mountains and the sea in the distance. Evening sky with clouds.

Bought from Mr. Farrer, 1855.
Exhibited—Royal Academy, 1871, No. 107.

FRANCIA (FRANCESCO RAIBOLINI), 1450 (?)-1517.

181   1. LUCRETIA.

Panel. 20½ × 16¾ in.

Half length, half life size. The head is slightly thrown back, the eyes looking up. She has light auburn hair, with a ruby ornament at the parting, and wears a loose robe of greyish blue. With her right hand she is plunging a dagger into her breast. There is a bracelet on her left arm. In the background a landscape, with two men on horseback, a monk, and three soldiers.

This picture was probably painted in the school of Francia. There are replicas, with some variations, in the Borghese Gallery at Rome (No. 64), in Mr. Solling's collection, and in the National Gallery of Ireland, No. 190.*

Bought from Mr. Martin Colnaghi.
Waagen, *Galleries*, 94.

---

* Vasari mentions a picture of Lucretia by Francia in the possession of the Duke Guido Baldo of Urbino.

182   2. HOLY FAMILY WITH ST. ANTHONY.

Panel.   12¼ × 10¼ in.

The Virgin sits in the centre on a wooden bench, with an apple in her left hand, and the infant Christ on her knees. Joseph stands on the left leaning on a stick, and St. Anthony of Padua on the right with a crucifix in his right hand. A hilly landscape in the background. The nimbus of Christ is of rays; those of the other figures are outline circles. They are gilt, as are the borders of the dresses, the crucifix, and the herbs in the foreground. Underneath, in gilt letters, is inscribed—

F.FRANCIA.AURIFEX.FACIEBAT.ANNO.MDXII.

This picture is in the style of Francesco Francia. The execution is very careful and minute, especially in the drawing of the hands, but not in that of the landscape, which is rather primitive. The somewhat heavy colouring makes it probable that it is a work of Giacomo, son and scholar of Francesco, who lived from about 1486 to 1557. No works of this artist, however, have as yet been found with an earlier date than 1518. The gilding of the inscription on the picture has been renewed without leaving any traces of its original form.

Bought from Mr. Farrer, 1855.

Waagen, *Galleries*, 94. "A very pretty and careful picture. From the colour of the gold I consider the inscription not to be genuine, and the picture rather by the hand of his son, Giacomo Francia."

Crowe and Cavalcaselle, i. 573.

GAROFALO (BENVENUTO TISIO), 1481–1559.

183   1. RIPOSO.

Panel.   14 × 19¾ in.

The Virgin, in a dark red dress and a blue mantle lined with violet, sits by a small marble table with her right hand resting upon an open book.   Behind her, to the right, near the base of two large columns, St. Anne, in a white mantle, is coming down some steps. On the left, Joseph, seated, raises the Infant with both hands from a cradle on which he stands.   Beyond is a balustrade, and the view of a sea-coast with a town and some high rocks.   Evening sky.

This is probably an early work of the master.   The representation of Joseph supporting the infant Christ is very seldom met with in Italian pictures.

Collection—Mr. Samuel Rogers,
Bought May 3, 1856, No. 701, £300.

184
2. ST. JAMES.

Panel. 19¾ × 15¾ in.

The Saint is represented standing in the act of preaching. His left arm is raised ; his right hand rests on a book, which lies on a small marble table decorated with a sphinx and rams' heads. A pilgrim's staff leans against his left shoulder. In the background is a large open window, in front of which a nun is kneeling. Some blue mountains and a town beyond.

This picture was formerly supposed to represent St. John the Evangelist at Patmos, but the pilgrim's staff makes it more probable that the Saint represented is St. James. The nun is probably a portrait of the person for whom the picture was painted. The landscape is probably a view of the Monti Eugenei, near Este, on the road from Ferrara to Padua.

Collection—Sir Thomas Baring.
Waagen, *Treasures*, ii. 176. He erroneously calls it "St. John the Baptist."

LUCA GIORDANO, 1632–1705.

185
ST. MICHAEL.

Canvas. 67 × 57 in.

The Archangel stands with his right foot on the breast of a fallen angel, whose body he pierces with a lance. Behind is another fallen angel with a serpent round his right arm. Below is the head of a dragon. Signed IORDANVS F. 1666.

Luca, *fa presto*, took for his model the celebrated pictures of the same subject by Raphael in the Louvre (No. 370), and by Guido Reni in the Church of St. Maria della Concezione at Rome. A similar picture by him is in the Belvidere Gallery at Vienna.

Collections—Sir Francis Baring.
　　　　　Sir Thomas Baring.
Exhibited—British Institution, 1840, No. 61.

GIORGIONE (GIORGIO BARBARELLI), (ASCRIBED TO),
1477–1511.

186   SALOME WITH THE HEAD OF ST. JOHN
THE BAPTIST.

From Panel transferred to Canvas. 31½ × 29 in.

Figures half length, life size. The head of Salome is turned a
little to the left. She wears a white bodice, with a pink scarf and
violet mantle. The Baptist's head in a dish rests upon her arms.
Behind her, to the left, is a maid-servant with black hair and green
dress.

This picture has been ascribed to various masters by high authorities. Passavant considered it a genuine Giorgione, as did Waagen
in 1835, but in 1857 he ascribed it to Vicenzio Catena. Crowe and
Cavalcaselle call it a replica by Pordenone, and Mündler considered
it to be "an original by Sebastiano del Piombo, or by Giorgione."

It is, in our opinion, an exact ancient replica of a picture in the
Doria Palace at Rome, ascribed by the catalogue to Pordenone, as
also by Crowe and Cavalcaselle ; to Romanino by Mündler ; while
Iwan Lermolieff[*] has rightly stated that it is an early work of
Titian, similar in style to the "Amor Divino ed Amor Profano" in
the Gallery Borghese at Rome.

Collection—Sir Thomas Baring.
Waagen, *Art and Artists*, iii. 35.
    „   *Treasures*, ii. 179.
Crowe and Cavalcaselle, ii. 287.
Burkhardt, *Cicerone*, Leipzig, 1874, 1086.
Passavant, i. 280.
Viardot, 154.
Exhibited—British Institution, 1840, No. 65.
        Manchester, 1857, No. 251.
Photographed, *Northbrook Gallery*.

* "Die Galerien Roms," in the "Zeitschrift für bildende Kunst," vol. xi. p. 135.

GUERCINO DA CENTO (GIOVANNI FRANCESCO BARBIERI), 1590-1666.

187   SEMIRAMIS RECEIVING NEWS OF THE REVOLT OF BABYLON.

Canvas.   50 × 58½ in.

Figures three-quarters length, life size. Semiramis stands to the left, her face seen in profile, in a rich amber-coloured brocade skirt, full white sleeves with gold stripes, and an embroidered low red bodice. Her right hand rests on the arm of a chair behind her, and her left arm is held out. Her fair hair hangs down her back and is being dressed by her maid, who stands behind her with a comb. A mirror and a crown are on a table before her. A messenger advances from the right, pointing backwards with his right hand; he holds his hat in his left hand, and is dressed in an amber doublet and dark hose.

A later work of the artist, painted under the influence of Guido. The composition resembles Guercino's representation of the same subject, painted for Cardinal Cornaro at Venice, now in the Dresden Gallery (No. 511). But in it Semiramis is sitting in the chair with the crown on her head. Another picture of the same subject is at Petworth (No. 155).

Collections—Haldemand.
       Mr. R. Sanderson.
Bought March 20, 1858, No. 19, £210.

188   2. THE SICK CHILD.

Panel.   8¼ × 11¼ in.

Figures three-quarters length.   A doctor sits to the right with
his right hand raised up, and some medicine in his left.   Opposite
him a woman holds her arms round a girl of about eight years of
age, who is struggling to avoid taking the physic.   Near by stands
another girl with a cup in her hand, and the head of an old woman
is seen to the left.

Scenes of popular life like that represented here by Guercino are
very seldom to be met with in pictures by Bolognese artists.   The
taste for them was, however, propagated in Italy, during the middle
of the seventeenth century, by wandering Dutch artists—Gerard van
Houthard, Pieter de Laar, Lingelbach, Weeninx, Karel Dugardin,
and others; and this somewhat exceptional picture was doubtless
executed under some such influence.

Collections—Laborde.
            Sir Francis Baring.
            Sir Thomas Baring.
Exhibited—British Institution, 1840, No. 31.

LIONARDO DA VINCI (ASCRIBED TO), 1452 1519.

189   BUST OF CHRIST.

Panel.   16½ × 13 in.

Life size, turned to the right; brown hair falling in curls over the shoulder; short beard. Reddish-brown garment, red mantle. The right hand is raised in benediction.

This picture has been traditionally ascribed to Lionardo, and in its general conception his influence is certainly perceptible; but the tone of the colouring and the expression more probably denoted it to have been painted by an unknown Milanese artist of the seventeenth century. A similar picture ascribed to Lionardo was in the Coesvelt Gallery (No. 93). In it Christ points with his right hand to an emblematic triangle. Another picture of the same class ascribed to Lionardo is in the Brignole Palace at Genoa.

Collections—Le Brun.
    Sir Thomas Baring.
Le Brun, i. 5. Engraved No. 2. "J'ai fait diminuer la planche des deux tiers, pour diminuer la masse de vers qui rongnait le bois."

LOMBARD SCHOOL.

190   MARTYRDOM OF ST. SEBASTIAN.

Panel.   11 × 30½ in.

Full-length figures, small. St. Sebastian, with a white cloth round his loins, is standing in the centre, his hands tied behind him to a leafless tree. To the right stands a person in authority, with his right hand stretched out in the act of commanding, and three men near him. Opposite are three archers, two of whom are shooting arrows at the Saint. In the background there is a palace in ruins, in front of which are two marble columns and the fragment of an altar. Two soldiers stand before the building, near a group of three cypress trees. There are two columns, decorated with shields, on either side of the picture.

This picture has been attributed to Raphael, but certainly without sufficient reason. The colouring, and the style of the architecture in the background, seem to indicate that it was painted by an artist of the Lombard school at the beginning of the sixteenth century. The panel originally formed part of a "cassone." The armorial bearings on the shields are not sufficiently well preserved to be identified.

Collection—Lord Northwick.
Bought July 28, 1859, No. 240, £92, 8s.

BERNARDINO LUINI, 1470-1530.

191   HOLY FAMILY.

Panel.   4½ × 33¾ in.

Full-length figures, half life size. The Virgin, seated with her head turned to the right, holds upon her knees the infant Christ, to whom St. John, who kneels on the right, presents a flower. Outline nimbi round the heads. Dark background.

A similar composition is in the Munich Gallery, engraved by Strixner, 1820.

Collection—Sir Thomas Baring.
Waagen, *Treasures*, ii. 178.

ANDREA MANTEGNA, 1430-1506.

192   CHRIST'S AGONY IN THE GARDEN.

Panel.   24½ × 31½ in.

A rocky hill, with a rough flight of steps, fills the centre and left of the picture. There Christ is represented kneeling, turned to the left, with his hands joined in prayer. He is dressed in a bluish-green mantle, which shows a small portion of a vermilion under-garment. Over his head, which is covered with fair curls, there is a nimbus with a red cross; his feet are bare. Opposite him, five boy angels stand on light clouds bearing the emblems of the Passion. A path-way winds round the foot of the hill, under which the three Apostles lie asleep. On the left, St. Peter, with grey hair, arms folded, blue under-garment, and carmine mantle ; on the right, St. James, with his left arm resting on a book, yellow under-garment, and violet mantle; his head rests on the thigh of St. John, who is clad in a red under-garment and green mantle. Round their heads are yellow nimbs. The brook Cedron flows in front of the path, with the hewn trunk of a tree placed over it as a bridge. On the right is a laurel tree with a raven perched upon it. Two herons are wading in the brook, and two hares are sporting on the hill; three more are on the path. In the background is seen the city of Jerusalem, behind high walls, on a rocky eminence. A procession is issuing from one of the gates, headed by Judas Iscariot, with Roman soldiers carrying lances and shields, and other persons, forming a crowd of miniature figures. Three steep rocks, one of them crowned with a ruined castle, rise behind the town. A green mountain landscape of Italian character is seen to the right. The very dark blue sky, broken by light clouds, indicates the late hour of the day.

Some of the buildings in the town are taken from well-known edifices of the time. The principal tower is a copy of the Torre di Nerone, on the Mons Viminalis, at Rome. In the interior is a building which resembles the arena of Verona, and a column, like Trajan's at Rome, on which is placed the bronze equestrian statue of Gattamelata by Donatello.* Near it is a hall like the Palazzo della Ragione in Padua. The towers resemble the pictures of ancient Padua, the highest of them especially that of St. Justinia; four are crowned with a gilt crescent.

The picture is signed, on the rock below Christ :

OPVS ANDREAE MANTEGNA

---

* Erasmus da Narni, called Gattamelata, was commander-in-chief of the army of the Republic of Venice (1438-1441). It was by order of the Republic that Donatello (Donato di Niccolo di Betti Bardi, 1386-1466) of Florence executed the equestrian statue, the first great bronze statue of modern art in Italy (1445). Set up in Padua on the Piazza del Santo, it was extolled as a first-rate work of art in the "Trattato di M. Francesco Bocchi" (1584); and its praises were sung by Pomponius Gauricus, "De Sculptura" (cf. Hans Semper, "Donatello," Wien, 1875, pp. 194 and 254). Until now no mention has been made of Donatello's bronze statue having been gilt, as it is shown by this earliest representation. The original in Padua is engraved in the "Guida di Padova Cittadella, &c.," Padova, 1842, p. 105.

Mantegna, who was an independent artist at Padova when only seventeen years of age, painted this picture when he was twenty-eight years old; it was executed in the year 1459 for Giacomo Marcello, Podesta of Padua, simultaneously therefore with the altar-piece of St. Zeno in Verona, where, on the predella, Mantegna treated the same subject, but with a different arrangement of the figures. The predella picture, representing Christ's Agony, is now in the Museum at Tours (26½ × 36½ in.).

The colouring of the picture is very powerful, and of a deeper tone than in the later works of the master. Its chief merit lies in its drawing and in its plastic forms, the smallest detail being executed with minute care.

The importance of the picture for the history of North Italian painting is quite unique, on account of the inferences which can be drawn from it as to the relations of Mantegna with the Venetian school. There is a drawing (p. xxxxiiii.) with the representation of the same subject in the sketch-book of Jacobo Bellini of Venice (c. 1400–1464), now in the British Museum. The conception is so much like that in this picture, that the connection between the two cannot be doubted.* Mantegna married Niccalosia Bellini, daughter of the painter Gentile Bellini, and grand-daughter of Jacobo Bellini. The date of this marriage cannot be fixed, but it is probable that it took place in 1450. We may therefore conclude that when Mantegna painted his picture, "Christ's Agony in the Garden," Giovanni Bellini, brother of Gentile (1427–1516), must have been in relation with him. This is, moreover, proved by the representation of the same subject by Giovanni Bellini in the National Gallery (No. 726), a picture which, in its conception as well as in its execution, entirely depends on that of Mantegna.

There is an ancient Italian drawing, No. 354 in the Malcolm

---

* The composition of Jacobo Bellini is divided into two parts : to the right, the sleeping apostles ; towards the centre, turned to the disciples, Christ kneeling on a rock ; the cup is placed on the mountain-top before him. On the left, Jerusalem ; soldiers marching out of a town-gate on a winding pathway. On the left, a high tree, the brook Cedron, with a bridge, and a monumental column. The age of the sketch-book is fixed by the handwriting on it, which runs : "De mano di me Jacobo Bellino, Veneto, 1430, in Venetia." Consult J. P. Richter, *Italian Art in the National Gallery*, London, 1883, p. 78.

Collection, representing Judas heading the band of Jews and soldiers. It is exactly the same group as in Mantegna's picture. This drawing, on which is noted "Carpazzo" (= Carpaccio), is ascribed by the catalogue of the Malcolm Collection (p. 127) to the "early Venetian school." An illuminated missal in Lord North-brook's collection gives the picture with some variations.

Mantegna's predella picture, "Christ's Agony in the Garden," originally in the Church of St. Zeno at Verona, and now in the Museum of Tours, is altogether different in its composition.

See "Notice des Tableaux du Musée du Département d'Indre et Loire," à Tours, 1838, p. 76, No. 179 :—"Jésus au Jardin des Olives. Jésus à genoux, les mains jointes, est appuyé sur un rocher; *il fixe l'ange qui lui apporte le calice d'amertume.* Sur le premier plan, les apôtres sont endormis ; on aperçoit à *gauche* dans le lointain, Judas Iscariott accompagné des soldats envoyés par les princes, des prêtres, les pharisiens, les scribes et les séna-teurs. Dans le fond, à gauche, on a représenté la ville de Jérusalem.

"Les détails de cette partie du tableau sont d'un travail et d'un fini admirables, quoique secs."

The picture at Tours is also described by Le Brun ; "Andrea Mantegna im Museum zu Tours" in Von Lützow's "Zeitschrift für bildende Kunst," vol. x. pp. 190, 191 ; by Clement de Riz, "Les Musées de Province," Paris, 1859, vol. i. pp. 272, 315 ; and in the *Times*, October 21, 1882.

An exceedingly rare engraving, after the picture at Tours, by Giacinto Maina, is in the print-room of the Berlin Museum.

Collections—Cardinal Fesch.
　　　　　Mr. Coningham.
Bought June 9, 1849, No. 58, £420.
Waagen, *Treasures,* ii. 178.
Crowe and Cavalcaselle, i. 141, 382, &c.
Burger, *Trésors d'Art exposés à Manchester,* Paris, 1857, 70–72.
Viardot, 153.
Kugler, *Handbook* (Layard), i. 286. "A marvellous combination of the fan-tastic and the realistic, with fine drawing, foreshortening, and drapery in the figures of the sleeping apostles."
Exhibited—Manchester, 1857, No. 98.
　　　　　Royal Academy, 1870, No. 58.

LODOVICO MAZZOLINI, 1481–1528.

193 INFANT CHRIST WITH THE DOCTORS IN
THE TEMPLE.

Panel. 17¼ × 12¼ in.

Christ is sitting on an elevated seat to the right, clad in a dark red garment and blue mantle, round his head a gilt nimbus, his right hand outstretched. To the left, opposite him, eight Jewish doctors sitting and disputing, some of them holding books; to the right, two others. In the foreground an ape approaching a boy, who holds an awl. To the left, in the background, the Virgin and Joseph are entering the Temple. In a gallery are five Jews, one of whom is handing down a roll of parchment to a man below. In all there are twenty figures. In the architectural background are two twisted columns; above, a relief with the representation of Roman soldiers on horseback fighting; below, a tablet with an inscription in Hebrew, the translation of which is, "The house which Solomon has erected to Jehovah."

Mazzolini was a scholar of Lorenzo Costa of Ferrara. Senor Giovanni Morelli calls him the "glowworm" of the Ferrarese school, and, as he has lately been recognised to have been one of the masters who influenced Correggio, his works have assumed a special interest in art history.

Hebrew inscriptions are very often to be met with on pictures by Mazzolini, and occasionally on pictures by Lorenzo Costa and other Ferrarese artists. It was just at that time that attention was directed to the study of Hebrew, and Jews were freely tolerated, especially at Ferrara.[*] The architecture in the buildings of the background is taken from the old Roman temples, and scarcely gives the impression of a Jewish temple. The gallery may be an imitation of a synagogue cathedra. The twisted columns are certainly copied from a unique monument at Rome, generally believed

---

* See Graet's "Geschichte der Juden," 2d edition, vol. vii. p. 171.

to have been brought from the Temple of Jerusalem, which during the Middle Ages supported the ciborium of the Basilica of St. Peter.

Lanzi says that a picture by Mazzolini representing the same subject was formerly in the cathedral of St. Francesco at Ferrara, and Cittadella further mentions it as adorning a chapel near the portal. According to Lanzi, this picture was originally united with another panel, representing the Nativity of Christ, bearing the inscription and the date "MDXXIII, *Zenar* (January), *Ludovicus Mazzolinus Ferrariensis.*" It is not known where this panel is now to be found.

The above-described picture is in the Berlin Gallery, No. 273 (panel, 18¼ × 11⅞ in.). It was formerly in the Giustiniani Palace at Rome, whilst the replica in Lord Northbrook's collection is said to come from the Aldobrandini collection at Rome, and to have been painted for a Cardinal Alessandro Aldobrandini, who was legate at Ferrara in the time of Mazzolini.

Collections—Villa Aldobrandini, Rome.
        Mr. William Young Ottley. Sold May 16, 1801, No. 11, £180.
        Mr. Samuel Rogers.
Bought May 3, 1856, No. 724, £525.
Lanzi, *Storia Pittorica,* Firenze, 1821, vol. v. p. 194.
G. Baruffaldi, *Vite de' pittori Ferraresi,* Ferrara, 1844, vol. i. p. 128.
C. Cittadella, *Catalogo istorico de pittori Ferraresi,* Ferrara, 1782, vol. i. p. 97.
Buchanan, ii. 22.
Mrs. Jamieson, *Companion to the Private Galleries,* London, 1844, p. 396.
Waagen, *Galleries,* 93.
Exhibited—Royal Academy, 1872, No. 218.

———————

ANTONIO RAFFAELLE MENGS, 1728–1779.

194   PORTRAIT.

Canvas. 26 × 19½ in.

Bust of a young lady, life size, three-quarters face, turned to the left. Red hair. Light blue dress. Two rows of pearls round her neck.

Collection—Sir Thomas Baring.

PIETRO FRANCESCO MOLA, 1612-1688.

195   1. HAGAR AND ISHMAEL.

Canvas.   17½ × 21 in.

Hagar kneels to the left, looking up, with outstretched arms, in
an attitude of despair.   The boy Ishmael lies on the ground before
her.   Above, on a cloud, is an angel pointing upwards with one
hand, and to some water, on the right, with the other.   Woody
landscape ; evening sky.

The representation of Hagar and Ishmael was a favourite one
with Mola.   Similar pictures by him are in the Louvre (No. 266)
and the Dulwich Gallery (No. 195).

Collections—Earl of Carysfort.
          Mr. Samuel Rogers.
Bought May 3, 1856, No. 688, £80, 2s.

196   2. RIPOSO.

Copper.   9 × 11¾ in.

The Virgin is seated in the centre of a woody landscape, with
the infant Christ in her lap, holding an apple.   The infant St. John
stands on the left, taking a cup from the Virgin.   To the right is
Joseph.   The figures are dramatically grouped and of tender expression.

Collection—Sir Thomas Baring.
Exhibited—British Institution, 1840, No. 4.

GIOVANNI BATISTA MORONI, 1510-1578.

197 PORTRAIT.

Canvas. 43 × 35 in.

Three-quarters length figure, life size, turned to the left, of a man in armour; full round face, short brown hair and beard. His left hand rests on his sword, his right on his helmet, which stands on a pillar. The branch of a palm, a grey wall, and brickwork in the background. Above, to the left, blue sky with a few clouds. Inscribed on the pillar—

MARIVS · BENVEN^{TVS}

SVB · CAROLO

IMPERAT · DVX.^{ORE}

According to the inscription, this picture represents Marius Benvenutus, a general during the reign of the Emperor Charles the Fifth; but the researches made for the purpose of identifying this personage have not led to any result. The name is not mentioned by the historians and biographers who have studied the period. From the features of the portrait, however, one may conclude that he was an Italian.

This picture, which is of a fine greyish harmony, must have been painted in the artist's middle life, and is perfectly well preserved.

Collection—King of Holland.
Sold August 1850, No. 168, 750 francs, to Mr. Chaplin.
Bought from Mr. Chaplin, 1850.
Waagen, *Galleries*, 95. "The action easy, and the animated head coloured and conceived much in the feeling of his master, Moretto. The hands of great truth, and the armour of masterly treatment."

PALMA VECCHIO (ASCRIBED TO).

198 HOLY FAMILY, ST. CATHARINE, AND ST. MARY MAGDALEN.

Canvas. 45 × 66½ in.

The Virgin is seated in the centre, wearing a crimson dress and a white hood. She holds on her knee the infant Christ, who stretches out his right hand towards a vase offered by Mary Magdalen, who kneels to the left. To the right St. Catharine sits with her right hand resting on the fragment of a wheel. Behind them is Joseph, and in the background a ruin, with a tower and mountains with some figures.

Although this picture has been ascribed to Palma Vecchio,[*] its conception and execution indicate it to be a work of one of the younger members of the Bonifacio family. The eldest painter of this name, Bonifacio I. Veronese, was a scholar and imitator of Palma Vecchio, to whom this picture was formerly attributed. But Palma Vecchio, who was a master of Titian, died in 1528, whilst most of the pictures hitherto attributed to him are painted in a manner peculiar to the artists of the second half of the sixteenth century. According to Cesare Bernasconi,[†] Bonifacio I. Veronese

---

[*] In the Catalogue of Sir John Murray's sale is the following description of the picture:—

"It was purchased in a selection of pictures from Sir Thomas Baring's collection during his lifetime. This picture, a valuable example of this master's works, is rendered still more so from containing four of the portraits of the family of the artist. The Virgin and Child are portraits of his wife and infant son. The Magdalen is the portrait of Violante, the mistress of Titian, while the male portrait is that of himself. That of the other figure is unknown. It is signed with large initials and dated. Original drawings of the Madonna, and of Violante as the Magdalen, are in the Imperial Collection at Vienna."

[†] "Studii sopra la storia della pittura italiana." Verona, 1864, pp. 237, 248.

died in 1540, Bonifacio II. Veneziano in 1553, Bonifacio III. Veneziano was still living in 1579. The two younger ones were both
scholars and imitators of Bonifacio I. Veronese, whose best production in England is a picture at Hampton Court, representing Diana
and Actæon in a fanciful landscape, erroneously ascribed to Giorgione (No. 73). The picture described above is, to judge by its
style,* a work of Bonifacio III. Veneziano. This painter was also
under the influence of Titian. In this picture, however, the influence of Palma Vecchio is also seen, especially in the drawing of the
hands.

The general arrangement of the compositions painted by the two
younger Bonifacii is very similar. They mostly introduce in the
foreground, as is the case here, a group of more than half life-size
figures, with a view of an extensive landscape on either side.

Collections—Sir Thomas Baring. Sold to Mr. Holford, 1843.
        Mr. W. Buchanan.
        General Sir John Murray.
Bought June 19, 1852, No. 49, £252.
Bryan, *Dictionary, &c.*, 1849, p. 534.
Waagen, *Art and Artists*, iii. 35.
Crowe and Cavalcaselle, ii. 486. "A genuine Bonifacio."
Exhibited—British Institution, 1840, No. 28.

----

* O. Mundler, "Beiträge zu Burckhardt's Cicerone." Leipzig, 1874, pp. 110, 111.
Iwan Lermolieff, "Die Galerien Roms," in the "Zeitschrift für bild. Kunst," vol. xi. pp.
136, 137.

PIETRO PAOLINI, 1603-1681.

199 VIRGIN AND CHILD, WITH ST. CATHERINE.

Canvas. 51½ × 39 in.

Full-length figures, life size. The Virgin is seated, in a red dress, blue mantle, and dark blue headdress with golden embroidery. She holds the Infant seated upright on her knees. He is placing the ring on St. Catherine's finger, who kneels opposite him, in a rich embroidered amber dress and violet mantle; near her on the ground lies a sword. Behind her St. Anne stands, holding a stick and a book. To the left an angel holds the crown of St. Catherine. A column, a dark green curtain, and an extensive landscape form the background. Signed on St. Anne's headdress.

Pietro Paolini of Lucca was a scholar of A. Carovelli. He was born in 1603 (as Lanzi says) or in 1604 (Baldinucci). He imitated Pordenone and P. Veronese. In this picture, executed with the greatest care, the influence of Caravaggio is perceptible in the rendering of light and shadow. The picture is said to have been painted for the city of Lucca.

Collections—Lucca Gallery.
  Sir Thomas Baring.
  Waagen, *Galleries*, 94, attributes this picture to Rondani, and says, "I know not on what authority it is given to Pietro Paolini, who painted, as far as his works are known to me, in a very different manner." He did not observe the signature, and the criticism is an example of the value of conjectural remarks upon Italian pictures, when made even by the most careful observers.

ITALIAN.

PARMEGIANO (FRANCESCO MAZZUOLI), 1503–1540.

200   HOLY FAMILY.

Panel.   62 × 46½ in.

Full-length figures, life size. In the centre the Virgin is seated, holding in her lap the infant Christ, who presents a swallow to the infant St. John, who sits to the left in his mother's lap. In the background are Joseph and an angel. In the foreground St. John's cross, round which is a scroll with the inscription : ECCE AGNUS DEI. The figures have outline nimbs round their heads.

This composition clearly betrays the manner of Parmegiano, but the drawing is in various parts inaccurate, and the colour less bright than is usual in his works.

Collection—Sir Thomas Baring.
Passavant, i. 281.
Waagen, *Art and Artists*, iii. 36.
    „   *Treasures*, ii. 178.
Exhibited—British Institution, 1816, No. 63.

SEBASTIANO DEL PIOMBO (FRA SEBASTIANO LUCIANI), 1485–1547.

201   HOLY FAMILY, WITH A DONOR.

Panel. 38¼ × 42 in.

Figures three-quarters length, small life size. In the centre the Virgin, seated, clad in a pink dress with a white scarf round the waist, bluish-green mantle lined with orange, and white headdress, holds the shoulder of the infant Christ with her left hand. He is turned to the left; his left knee rests on her lap, whilst his right leg is stretched forward; he appears as if about to descend and bless the donor, whom the Virgin is presenting to him. The donor, a half-length figure of a man about forty years of age, is in adoration with his hands crossed on his breast, his face turned upwards; he has long black hair and a black beard. To the right is Joseph in an orange-coloured dress, leaning on a table, asleep. To the left, behind the donor, is St. John the Baptist, a young man covered with a camel-skin, a cross resting on his right shoulder. A green curtain is behind the head of the Virgin. Dark background.

Sebastiano was a scholar of Giovanni Bellini, and became a follower of Giorgione, but when he settled at Rome he attached himself to Michael Angelo, and giving up for some time (about 1515–1525) his Venetian traditions of colour, he became an interpreter of Michael Angelo's grand artistic principles. The described picture belongs to the beginning of this Michaelangelesque period. In its style it comes very near to the " Resurrection of Lazarus," No. 1 in the National Gallery, painted in 1518 and 1519. In its composition it is even more imposing, and in its drawing more studied and nobler.

Collections—Senatore Cambiaso, Genoa.
          Le Brun.
          Sir Thomas Baring. Sold to Mr. Coningham, 1843.
          Mr. Coningham.

(131)

ITALIAN.

Bought June 9, 1840, No. 61, £1800.

Le Brun, i. 37. Engraved, No. 21. "Le tableau offre la composition de Michel Ange et ses contours, la couleur et le fini harmonieux des plus parfaits ouvrages de Léonard de Vinci. Je ne crains pas de dire que c'est un des premiers chefs-d'œuvre de l'art ; il sort de la magnifique collection du sénateur Cambiaso à Gênes ; et ce n'est qu'avec beaucoup de peines que j'ai pu obtenir qu'il me le cédât."

Buchanan, ii. 263.

Passavant, i. 279. "This very splendid picture is so grand, alike in arrangement and design, that it gives rise to the surmise of its having been executed from a cartoon by Michael Angelo. The colouring altogether is powerful and warm ; the head of the Virgin is however too dark and brown."

Waagen, *Art and Artists*, iii. 33 ; *Treasures*, ii. 175. "A *chef-d'œuvre* of Sebastien del Piombo, in which the spirit of Michael Angelo and his own admirable style of art are united in the happiest way, represents the Florentine School in its highest development. . . . In treatment and in tone, this picture shows a close affinity to the 'Raising of Lazarus,' being decidedly painted about the same time ; while it may be considered, after that, as the most valuable specimen in England of this master."

Crowe and Cavalcaselle, ii. 325, 326. "Two works of uncommon beauty were, we should think, completed at this juncture—when Sebastian composed pictures under the guidance of Michael Angelo—the 'Holy Family' of the Baring Collection, and the 'Pietà' of the Hermitage at Petersburg. Even at this time, as we judge from the Baring masterpiece, Venetian elements still outweighed the Florentine in Sebastian's manner. The very form of his composition scents of the Bellinesque. A donor, with his arms piously crossed over his breast, kneels before the Virgin, who kindly rests one hand on his shoulder, whilst with the other she guides the stride of the infant Christ upon her lap. To the left, the Baptist, with his cross, contemplates the scene. To the right, St. Joseph sleeps. A green curtain hangs behind the group. The donor and the Baptist are most Venetian, the Saviour and St. Joseph most Florentine ; but the study of Tuscan art is displayed to a considerable extent in the type and movement, in the setting of drapery to show the under surfaces, and in broad general treatment. There is more skill in the composition than Sebastian had hitherto shown, more firmness and decision in outline, and a grander, truer rendering of extremities. The colour is tinged in a slight degree with the leaden shade peculiar to Sebastian's later creations, and the glowing richness of a Northern palette is tempered by sober yet admirable chiaroscuro."

W. Burger, *Trésors d'Art exposés à Manchester en 1857*, Paris, 1857, p. 43.

Kugler, *Handbook* (Layard), ii. 562.

Viardot, 154.

Exhibited—British Institution, 1816, No. 7, and 1840, No. 63.

> Manchester, 1857, No. 161. (See Waagen, *A Walk through the Art Treasures Exhibition at Manchester*, p. 10.)
>
> Royal Academy, 1870, No. 130.

RAFFAELLO SANZIO (ascribed to), 1483–1520.

202   1. VIRGIN AND CHILD.

Panel.   26 × 14½ in.

The Virgin, three-quarters length, less than life size, with very
fair hair, a white veil falling down over her left shoulder, pink
dress and violet scarf, is seated in front, with her head inclining a
little to the left. Her left hand rests in her lap upon a blue mantle
with a gilt border. The infant Christ stands on her knees, with
his left hand resting on her bosom, his head turned to the left.
There are nimbs over both heads, formed by double gilt circles.
Close behind the Virgin there is a low balustrade, and the background is composed of a hilly landscape, with some trees and a
farm to the right.

The picture, which traditionally bears the name of Raphael, has
been ascribed by Dr. Waagen and Messrs. Crowe and Cavalcaselle
to Lo Spagna and to Eusebio da San Giorgio, two of his scholars ;
but their works which are extant differ in style and are of less
merit. A replica or copy of this picture is, in the Munich Gallery,
erroneously ascribed to Fra Bartolommeo.[*]

The method of painting used in Lord Northbrook's picture appears
to resemble that of the "Entombment" in the Borghese Gallery at
Rome, and the "St. Catherine," No. 168, in the National Gallery,
both of which pictures were painted about the year 1507. It must
however be mentioned that the drawing does not entirely conform
to the idealistic conceptions of Raphael, the hands, for instance, being
too short ; but the same peculiarity may be observed in the earliest
of the two Panshanger Raphaels.

[*] Engraved by Lorenz Quaglia, 1818, in Stroxner and Piloty. Konigl. Bav.
Gemaldgallerie.

(153)   U

This picture also in many respects resembles one of a similar composition at Stafford House, erroneously ascribed to Luca Penni (Catalogue, No. 32). Perhaps both pictures may with some reason be ascribed to Timoteo Viti (1467–1523), an artist whose great merits have not yet been sufficiently appreciated.

Collections—Methuen. Catalogue of pictures at Corsham House by John Britton, 1806, No. 28. Sold in 1844 to Sir Thomas Baring.
            Sir Thomas Baring.
Waagen, *Treasures*, ii. 176.
Crowe and Cavalcaselle, iii. pp. 327, 342, 475.
Ruland, *Works of Raphael*, London, 1876, p. 84.
Kugler, *Handbook* (Layard), i. 245.
Photographed, *Northbrook Gallery.*

203   2. ST. JOHN THE BAPTIST PREACHING.

(COPY ASCRIBED TO GIULIO ROMANO.)

Panel. 34 × 27 in.

One of the many representations of this subject, the finest of which is in the Uffizi Gallery at Florence. This picture corresponds in every detail with the somewhat larger one sold in the Orleans Gallery. There is another rather smaller in the Grosvenor House Collection (Young's Catalogue, No. 49).

Collections—Marchese Guadagni, Florence.
            Sir Thomas Baring.

GUIDO RENI, 1575–1642.

204   1. ECCE HOMO.

Canvas.   42½ × 37 in.

Three-quarters length figure of Christ wearing the crown of thorns, bending forwards, with his arms crossed and a reed in his right hand. A purple mantle falls from his right shoulder, and is gathered round his loins, leaving the chest bare. Painted in a light silvery tone and with spirited execution.

Collections—Lucien Buonaparte.
            Sir Thomas Baring.

Buchanan, ii. 285. "A few pictures of a fine class were sold out of this collection (Lucien Buonaparte's) immediately on its being notified to be for sale, among which were the 'Ecce Homo' by Guido, purchased by Sir Thomas Baring for 400 guineas."

It is not included in the catalogue of the gallery published by Müller, London 1812, but is engraved by Folo in the illustrations.*

Waagen, Art and Artists, iii. 37.
    „   Treasures, ii. 180.
Passavant, i. 281.
Exhibited—British Institution, 1816, No. 33.

205   2. BUST OF THE VIRGIN.

Canvas.   10¾ × 16½ in.

Life size. The head turned upwards, both hands folded on the bosom. Golden-coloured background.

Collections—Chevalier Boucheron.
            Sir Thomas Baring. Bought from Mr. Buchanan.

---

* No. 117 in my copy, in the place of a Bronzino. The picture is No. 29 of the original catalogue. Buchanan, ii. 289.

GIOVANNI FRANCESCO ROMANELLI, 1617–1663.

206   EUROPA.

Canvas.   20½ × 24 in.

Europa is seated on the bull, decorated with flowers, surrounded by cupids and attendants.   The sea in the distance to the right; some trees to the left.

Bought 1854.

_____

SALVATOR ROSA (ASCRIBED TO), 1615–1673.

207   1. LANDSCAPE.

Canvas.   27¼ × 36½ in.

The shore of a river.   Mountains to the right.   In the foreground two soldiers and two men, three others and a boat beyond. Farther back, a round tower and other buildings on the shore.

208   2. ST. JOHN THE BAPTIST PREACHING.

Canvas.   28⅞ × 38 in.

To the right, St. John stands on the shore of a brook, a group of persons sitting or standing round him.   The scene is closed by high rocks and trees.

These pictures were probably painted in imitation of Salvator by a contemporary artist.

Collections—Lebrun.
         Sir Thomas Baring.
Lebrun, ii. 7.   Engraved, Nos. 121 and 123.
Waagen, Treasures, ii. 180.
One or both exhibited British Institution, 1840, No. 52, and 1844, No. 91.

ANDREA DEL SARTO (VANNUCHI), 1487-1531.

209   1. ST. JOHN THE BAPTIST.

Panel.   26½ × 21½ in.

Half length, life size, turned to the left, about twenty years of age, with a cross in his right hand, and pointing with his left.   A red mantle is on his right arm, and a camel-skin hangs by a strap over his left shoulder round his hips.   Dark background.   This picture is of the artist's later period; it is broadly painted, with sharp outlines.

Collection—Sir Thomas Baring.
Waagen, *Treasures*, ii. 175.   " A very powerful study for a larger picture, in which, according to tradition, St. John is pointing to the Virgin and Child.'
Exhibited—British Institution, 1840.

210   2. VIRGIN AND CHILD.

Panel.   24 × 18½ in.

The Virgin standing, half length, less than life size.   Opposite her the infant Christ, seated on a white cushion with a gold border on a balustrade.   The Virgin looks fondly at the Child, and raises his face with her left hand, while her right rests on his back. He is dressed in a lemon-coloured tunic; the Virgin in a crimson dress and a pink kerchief falling down over her right shoulder. Dark background.

A replica of this picture is at Hampton Court, No. 282.   In it the child's tunic is violet, and the cushion has no gold border. Another, according to Crowe and Cavalcaselle (who attribute the picture to Domenico Puligo) is at Alnwick Castle.

Collections—Mr. Gray.
            Sir Thomas Baring.   Bought from Mr. Buchanan.
Waagen, *Treasures*, ii. 175.
Crowe and Cavalcaselle, iii. 584.

211   3. BUST OF A YOUNG MAN.

Panel.   10½ × 15½ in.

Life-size portrait of a young man with his head turned to the
left, long hair, dark eyes, regular features, wearing a three-cornered
hat and a bluish-black coat lined with fur.   Green background.

This portrait, said to be of one of the Medici family, was ascribed
to Raphael, but is more probably a work of Andrea del Sarto, to
whom it has also been ascribed by Dr. Gustavo Frizzoni of Milan.

Collections—Medici, Palazzo Riccardi, Florence.
            Le Brun.
            Sir Thomas Baring.
Le Brun, i. 65.   Engraved, No. 40, as by Raphael.
Buchanan, ii. 254.
Waagen, Art and Artists, iii. 35.
    „   Treasures, ii. 176, where he ascribes it to Pontormo.
Viardot, 154.
Exhibited—British Institution, 1824, No. 21, and 1840, No. 68.

SASSOFERRATO (GIUSEPPE SALVI), 1605–1685.

212   HOLY FAMILY.

Copper.   9½ × 13 in.

The Virgin is seated in the centre, in a pink dress, blue mantle,
and brown head-dress.   She holds up a white covering over the
infant Christ, who lies asleep on a grassy bank.   To the right
Joseph, to the left the infant St. John; some flowers and trunks
of trees behind him.   The motive of the central group is taken
from Raphael's so-called " Madonna di Loreto." An almost identical
composition, but larger, with some differences in the dress of the
figures, and with a cross lying on the bank in the foreground, is at
Chatsworth, attributed to Carlo Maratti.

Bought from Mr. Bentley, 1845.

BARTOLOMMEO SCHEDONE, 1506-1615.

213   1. HEAD OF A GIRL.

Panel.   Round.   6½ in. diameter.

About eight years old, face turned to the right. Black hair and white turban. Schedone has painted the same girl in a picture called " The Horn-Book," engraved in Tomkins' British Gallery, from the collection of Lord Ashburnham.

Collection—Sir Thomas Baring.
Exhibited—British Institution, 1840, No. 15.

214   2. ST. MARY MAGDALEN IN CONTEMPLATION.

Panel.   18 × 21½ in.

Seated, looking upwards, with her right arm on her knee and a handkerchief in her left hand. Reddish-brown dress and dark blue mantle. To the right is an angel boy sitting with his arms round a vase, and another to the left, standing behind, holding a skull, which rests on a book near which are some rosaries and chains. In the background dark clouds and two trees.

In this composition the artist comes near to Correggio. The distribution of deep shadows and bright light is of great effect.

It is not certain whether this picture is that which is engraved (No. 106) in the collection of Lucien Buonaparte, and described by Buchanan (ii. 272) as having been in the collection of the King of Naples at Capo di Monte, for the engraving does not quite correspond with the picture. There is another of the same subject, rather smaller (canvas, 15½ × 13 in.), at Grosvenor House, engraved in Young's " Illustrated Catalogue," No. 138. A similar composition by Schedone, but without the skull, is engraved by J. Pavon (18 × 13 in.).

Collection—Sir Thomas Baring. Bought from Mr. Buchanan.
Exhibited—British Institution, 1840.

215   3. RIPOSO.

(ASCRIBED TO.)

The Virgin, seated to the left, with the infant Christ before her, and St. John kneeling. Joseph is sitting to the right. An angel is lying down in a meadow in the background. Painted by an unknown Italian artist.

Collections—Le Brun.
           Sir Thomas Baring.
Le Brun, i, 101. Engraved, No. 84.

SOLARIO, ANTONIO (ascribed to), 1448-1500.

216   VIRGIN AND CHILD.   •

Panel. 13 × 11 in.

The Virgin, half length, in a violet head-dress, fair hair, with two long rather straight curls hanging on each side of her face, stands behind a balustrade upon which the infant Christ stands supported by her. He is raising his left hand in the act of blessing ; round his head is a radiating nimbus. To the left a green curtain forms the background, and to the right there is a distant view of a castle perched upon a rocky eminence.

This picture has been ascribed to A. Verrochio because of the inscription AVEROC on the border of the Virgin's dress. But, as pointed out by Crowe and Cavalcaselle, the letters were probably originally AVEMARIA. The gilding of the nimbs and borders of the dress show that the picture was painted early in the sixteenth century, and the long curls worn by the Virgin indicate its Lombard origin, for this was the fashion of the ladies of Lombardy at

(160)

that time. Crowe and Cavalcaselle were probably right in attributing it to A. Solario, called Del Gabba, of Milan, who was influenced by Lionardo and Antonello da Messina. Early works by him are rare. The landscape has much similarity to Albert Dürer.*

Collection—Mr. Harman.
Bought through Mr. Chaplin, 1851.
Crowe and Cavalcaselle, ii, 6².

TITIAN (TIZIANO VECELLIO), 1477-1576.

217 CHARLES V. ON HORSEBACK.

Canvas, 34 × 28½ in.

The Emperor, in armour and plumed helmet without visor, a red scarf over his left shoulder, and a lance in his right hand, is galloping on a black horse to the right. He is seated on a crimson saddle with a large reddish-brown saddle-cloth. To the left are trees, to the right a flat meadow. Cloudy morning sky.

In the year 1548 Titian visited Augsburg as court painter to Charles V. He writes † to his friend Pietro Aretino at Venice, April 1548, that his Majesty wishes to be painted by him on horseback, in the same armour he wore in the battle of Muhlberg on the 24th of April of the previous year. On the morning of the battle the Emperor mounted, according to contemporary records,‡ a dark Andalusian charger, covered with a red silk cloth with golden tassels. His helmet and his brilliant armour were also decorated with gold. Over it he wore a pink ribbon, the emblem of Commander of the House of Bourbon. In his right hand he held a spear. During the campaign the Emperor had suffered much from gout. His face was pale, and from his appearance he was even

---

* Dr. Schmarsow, Professor of Art History at the University of Breslau, was kind enough to look at this picture for me in 1887, and confirmed the opinion that it was painted by A. Solario. He considers it to be very like a large altar-piece by that artist in the Certosa di Pavia.—N.
† Lettere di Pietro Aretino, vol. iv, pp. 155, 202.
‡ Don Luis de Avola of Zúñigo, Comentario.

called by the Protestants "the ghost," "the embalmed corpse," and "the dead." But being desirous to take vengeance on his enemies, and trusting in the superiority of his army, he assumed the attitude of a cavalier as in his former days, in spite of his physical sufferings.

The various records of the Emperor's appearance in the battle all agree with the life-size equestrian portrait, painted by Titian, now in the Museo del Prado at Madrid No. 45.7). The above-described picture, which was formerly in the Orleans and in Mr. Rogers' collection, has the special value of being an exact copy of it. It only differs from it in the horsecloth, which here is not so finished in its details. Similar pictures, but different in size, are mentioned in the Catalogue of the Farnese Collection of 1680, and in the Catalogue of the Gallery of Queen Christina of Sweden.

Engraved by Massard, Orleans Gallery, vol. ii., Titian, No. 20.
Collections—Orleans. Sold for £150.
       Mr. Angerstein.
       Mr. Samuel Rogers.
Bought May 2, 1856, No. 619, £204, 15s.
Mrs. Jameson, *Companion to the Private Galleries in London*, 1844, p. 403.
Waagen, *Galleries*, 95.

TITIAN, or PARIS BORDONE.

218   PORTRAIT.

Canvas.   40 × 29½ in.

Three-quarters length figure, life size, of a dignified man, standing
looking to the left, with short black hair and beard; dressed in
black.   His left hand, with a ring on the forefinger, rests on his
hip; his right on a table, on which is an hour-glass.   Above, to
the left, is a niche containing two books, and a paper with the
inscription—

EST MORI NOBIS
DE CŒ DEBITV
(Est mori nobis de cœlo debitam.)

On the right, on the base of a column, is an inscription—

A . S . Æ . 37
(Anno suæ ætatis 37.)
MDXXI.

Mr. Smith sold this picture to Mr. Baring in 1853 as a work of
Titian, with the following note :—

"A portrait of a Venetian gentleman by Titian. This picture came from
the gallery of Godoy, Prince of Peace, First Minister of the Court of
Spain. It was imported into England at the commencement of the year
1815 by Mons. de Crochart, Paymaster of the French army in Spain, of
whom the late proprietor purchased it, with several other pictures from
the same collection, and sold it to me last month. From the date on the
picture I have reason to believe it to be the portrait of Andrea Navagero or
Naugerius."

Crowe and Cavalcaselle ascribe the picture to Pordenone, but we
are not acquainted with any authentic work by him which shows so

(163)

delicate a harmony of colour, and it may, with greater confidence, be ascribed to Paris Bordone, who was born at Treviso in 1500, went to Venice when eight years of age, and became, for a short time, a pupil of Titian, but afterwards adopted the style of Giorgione. In this picture the influence of Giorgione is pronounced, both in its conception and in the deep tones of the colouring. If rightly ascribed to Bordone, it is one of his most important works in his earliest manner. Pictures of this period by him are exceedingly rare; another, also a male portrait, is in Lady Eastlake's collection. The later style of Bordone, by which he is now chiefly known, is very different.

It is impossible to find out whether the statement of Mr. Smith that the picture is a portrait of Andrea Navagero was a traditional one, or was exclusively based upon the date.

Another picture of Navagero, half length, by Tintoretto, is engraved in outline in the *Annales du Musée*, Galerie Giustiniani, Paris, with the inscription ANDREAS NAUGERIUS. MDXXVI. on the base of a column of the same kind as that in the picture here described. The face is that of an older man, and the hair is worn long. The "anonimo di Morelli" describes a portrait of Navagero by Raphael, which, in the beginning of the sixteenth century, was in the house of Pietro Bembo of Venice. The original has been lost, but there are copies of it in the Palazzo Doria at Rome and the Museo del Prado at Madrid. We learn also from Sansovino that Titian introduced Navagero's portrait into his large historical paintings in the Sale del Maggior Consiglio of the Palazzo Ducale at Venice, which were destroyed by fire in 1577.

An engraving of his portrait, the head seen in profile, copied from a relief on a Paduan monument, is published as a frontispiece to the Paduan edition of his works.[*] Another engraved portrait, showing the head three-quarters in profile, is to be found in N. Reusner's "Icones."[†] There is certainly a great likeness between the features represented in these two engravings and those in this

---

[*] "Andreæ Naugerii, Patricii Veneti, Oratoris et Poetæ, Opera omnia," Venetia, 1613; Padova. 1718.

[†] Nicolaus Reusnerus, "Icones sive Imagines Vivæ Literis Cl. Virorum Italiæ Graeciæ, &c." Basileæ, 1589. 8vo.

picture, especially in the largeness of the face, the arched eyebrows, and the prominent cheek-bones.

The inscription, " Est mori nobis de cœlo debitum," and the hour-glass standing on the table, give additional ground for supposing the picture to be of Navagero, for on the 25th of June 1521, the year in which the picture was painted, he delivered the funeral oration on the Doge Leonardo Loredano.*

Collections—The Prince of Peace.
            M. de Crochart, 1815.
Bought of Mr. J. Smith, 1853.
Crowe and Cavalcaselle, ii. 290.
Exhibited—Royal Academy, 1871, No. 84.

* Andr. Navagero, "In Funere L. Lauredani," Venezia, 1613. Andrea Navagero or Naugerius, born in 1483, was one of the most distinguished Venetian scholars and statesmen of his day. In his youth he devoted himself to literary work, and became librarian of the Library of St. Mark. In 1523 he was sent to the Spanish court as ambassador of the Republic, and afterwards to the court of France, where he died at Blois in 1529.

PIERINO DEL VAGA, 1499–1547.

VIRGIN AND CHILD.

Panel.   41½ × 32 in.

The Virgin is seated, three-quarters length, life size, in a red
dress with yellow sleeves, and a blue mantle.   In her left hand she
holds some fruit, and with her right supports the infant Christ,
who is rising from a white cushion on her lap to throw his arms
lovingly round her neck.   In the background is a green curtain.

Pietro Buonacorsi (called Del Vaga) of Florence was one of
Raphael's best scholars, and after his death worked chiefly at
Genoa.   Most of his works are in fresco, and very few of his oil
paintings are known.   A large altar-piece of the Nativity, signed
with his full name and the date 1534, is in the collection of the
Earl of Dudley.   A comparison of the above-described picture with
this standard work shows that both are by the same hand and
belong to the same time of his life.   The shape of the Infant's
head, the graceful drawing of the mouth, the peculiar formation of
the hands, the choice of the colours, and the pronounced roundness
of the angle in the eyes in both pictures are almost identical.   This
picture comes from Genoa, where the most active part of the
painter's life was spent.

Collections—Senatore Cambiaso, Genoa.
           Le Brun.
           Sir Thomas Baring.
Le Brun, i. 67.   Engraved, No. 41, as by Giulio Romano.
Buchanan, ii. 254.   "One of the finest pictures at Stratton."
Passavant, i. 280.
Waagen, *Art and Artists*, iii. 35.
       "   *Galleries*, 94.   "This picture is original and attractive in motive,
           admirable in drawing, and of powerful warm brown tone of flesh ;
           but the shot stuffs, in the style of fresco-painting, are rather crude.
           Judging from conception, colouring, and treatment, I consider this
           to be a very good work by the hand of Perino del Vaga."
Exhibited—British Institution, 1816, No. 8, and 1840, No. 29.

PIERINO DEL VAGA (ASCRIBED TO).

220   BUST OF A YOUNG WOMAN.

Canvas. 21 × 15 in.

Life size, turned to the right. Fair hair, regular features, low green dress lined with blue. This picture, ascribed to Pierino del Vaga, was probably painted by a Florentine artist under the influence of Bronzino about the middle of the sixteenth century.

Collection—Sir Thomas Baring.

Waagen, *Treasures*, ii. 175, ascribes it to Sebastian del Piombo in his later time.

GIORGIO VASARI, 1512-1574.

221   1. ST. MARK.

Panel. 69½ × 38½ in.

Whole length, somewhat larger than life. The Saint is sitting, his head in profile, turned to the left, and holds his Gospel; a pair of eye-glasses are between the fingers of his right hand, and an inkstand and a pen in his left. In the foreground, to the right, is his emblem, the lion. On the book is inscribed ANGELUS DESCENDIT DEVO.

222   2. ST. LUKE.

Panel.   69½ × 38½ in.

The companion picture. The Saint sits to the right, his head in profile. His Gospel, in which he is writing, rests on his left knee; he holds an inkstand in his left hand. In the foreground, to the right, is his emblem, the bull.

The artist, in his comprehensive autobiography, does not mention that he painted figures of the Evangelists. But the style of these pictures perfectly agrees with that of his genuine works, and Vasari confesses that he was unable to enumerate all his productions.

Collection—Sir Thomas Baring.
Passavant, i. 283.
Waagen, *Art and Artists*, iii. 31.   "Extremely well-executed and well-coloured
         pictures. The designs borrowed from his master, Michael Angelo.
         St. Mark from the Sibylla Persica in the Sistine Chapel."
   „   *Treasures*, ii. 176.

PAOLO VERONESE (CALIARI), 1528–1588.

223   BAPTISM OF CHRIST.

Canvas.   41¼ × 31 in.

In the foreground, to the left, is a river, with a grassy bank to the right. Christ stands in the water, with white and violet drapery round his hips. He bends forward, with his hands crossed on his breast, while St. John, kneeling on his left knee, pours water from a vase over his head. There are small nimbs round the heads of both figures. A white dove, surrounded by a bright light, hovers over the baptismal vase. Near by, on the left, are the heads of two cherubim, and two angel boys above. The opposite bank of the river, with high trees, forms the background. Evening sky.

This picture is very like one by the same artist in the Pitti Gallery at Florence (No. 186).

Collections—Sir Joshua Reynolds. Sold March 1795, fourth day, No. 23,
          £25, 4s.
          Sir Francis Baring.
          Sir Thomas Baring.
Waagen, *Art and Artists*, iii. 36.
   „   *Treasures*, ii. 179.
Viardot, 154.
Exhibited—British Institution, 1840, No. 55.

SPANISH SCHOOL.

ALONZO CANO, 1601–1667.

224   VIRGIN AND CHILD.

Canvas. 43 × 34 in.

Three-quarters length, life size. The Virgin, with black hair, red dress, and blue mantle, is seated, bending forward looking at the child lying in her lap on white drapery.

Collection—Louvre, King Louis Philippe.
Bought May 13, 1853, No. 224, £200.
Waagen, *Galleries*, 96.

LUIS MORALES, 1509–1586.

225   1. ECCE HOMO.

Panel. 29 × 22 in.

Half length, life size. Christ standing, his head turned to the right, auburn hair, short beard; on his right shoulder a violet mantle, his chest uncovered; a reed in his left hand. To the right, Pilate, white beard, red hat, blue and red dress, with a baton in his left hand; his right points at Christ. Dark background. The design is very severe and precise, a peculiarity remarkable in the pictures by Morales, who frequently painted this subject.

Collection— Louvre, King Louis Philippe.
Bought May 13, 1853, No. 252, £110.

226   2. CHRIST BEARING THE CROSS.

Canvas.   26½ × 31 in.

Half length, life size.   Christ, with long fair hair, short beard, and violet dress, bends forward, the face turned to the front.   The cross rests upon his left shoulder and is supported by both hands. The crown of thorns is on his head.   Light from above.

This picture has been ascribed to Morales.   Waagen at first supposed it to be of his later period, but afterwards it has been, with more probability, ascribed, both by him and by Passavant, to an unknown Spanish artist of the seventeenth century.   Stirling (230) says that all Morales' pictures were painted on panel.

Collections—De Calonne.   Sold March 27, 1795, No. 31, £94, 10s.
                     Bryan.   Sold May 17, 1798, No. 45, £69, 6s.
                     Sir Francis Baring.
                     Sir Thomas Baring.
Buchanan, i. 244, 285.
Passavant, i. 283.   "Ascribed to Morales.   A fine Spanish picture, but of later date."
Waagen, Works of Art, iii. 41.
     „   Treasures, ii. 181.   "A good Spanish picture of the seventeenth century, noble in expression, and allied to Zurbaran in the subdued greyish tones."
Exhibited—British Institution, 1819, No. 60, and 1837, No. 28.

BARTOLOMÉ ESTÉBAN MURILLO, 1618-1682.

227   OUR LADY OF THE IMMACULATE CONCEPTION.

Canvas.   75 × 56¾ in.

Figures full length, small life size.   The Virgin, looking down with her hands joined in prayer, floats on a crescent in the clouds. She wears a white dress, an amber veil round her neck, and over her left arm a blue mantle, which falls behind to her right.   Round her head there is a silvery nimbus, composed of rays and of two large circles; on either side of it are six winged angels' heads on clouds.   Below are ten cherubs, one carrying a branch of palm (indicating her holiness), another a lily (her virginity), a third three roses (her beauty), a fourth a mirror (her freedom from all stain). There is a halo of bright light round the figure of the Virgin, and pale blue sky behind.

Murillo frequently painted this subject.   Perhaps the most celebrated of these works is the picture in the Louvre, bought by the French Government at Marshal Soult's sale in 1852 for 615,300 francs.   Another is at Lockinge.

Collections—Convent of Barefooted Carmelites, Calle de Alcala, Madrid.
          Le Brun.
          Sir Thomas Baring.
Le Brun, ii. 25.   Engraved, No. 134.
Buchanan, ii. 255.
Waagen, *Art and Artists*, iii. 41.
    „   *Treasures*, ii. 181.
Passavant, i. 283.
Blanc, *Histoire des Peintres*, Paris, 1869, Ecole Espagnole, 16.
Stirling, 1419.
Curtis, 131, No. 32, says the picture is mentioned by Cean Bermudez, *Diccionario*, ii. 63, and by Pons, *Viage*, v. 248.
Exhibited—British Institution, 1816, No. 46, and 1840, No. 92.
Engraved—M. S. Carmona, line, Madrid, 1802, 19·7 × 14·1 in. (Curtis).
          R. Graves, line, London, 1864, 20 × 15 in.
Photographed, *Northbrook Gallery.*

228   2. DON ANDRES DE ANDRADE.

Canvas. 77¾ × 46 in.

Full length, life size. Andrade was Pertigero or verger of the
cathedral at Seville. He has bushy black hair, and wears a dark
doublet with slashed sleeves, a linen collar, black breeches, and white
stockings. He holds a broad-brimmed hat in his left hand, while
his right rests on the head of a white-and-brown mastiff sitting by
his side. Behind him is a balustrade, and a square column on the
left ; on it is a coat of arms. On a bend dexter the figures of the
Virgin kneeling and the First Person of the Trinity. On a border
encircling the shield is the inscription, "*Ave Maria gratia (sic)
plena.*"

In the execution of this picture Murillo has applied a somewhat
different method than usual.

Mr. R. Ford, in the *Athenæum* of May 21, 1853, p. 623, gave
the following description of the picture :—

"The great picture of the day was a genuine portrait by Murillo of
Andres Andrade, the state verger of the Cathedral of Seville. It was
knocked down for £1020, amid the cheers of the competitors. . . . This
picture was purchased some twenty years ago at Seville by the late Sir
John Brackenbury, Consul at Cadiz, who obtained it from the heirs of
Andrade for less than £400. Some dispute arose between the agent
employed and Sir John, who refused him the usual fee ; thereupon the
broker gave information to the authorities,—the old law of Charles the
Third against the exportation of paintings was put in force,—and the
picture was embargoed. Some time after, a poor copy of the picture was
picked up,—leave was obtained to compare it with the original,—and the
copy was substituted in its place.

"Sir John subsequently would have sold his picture to the Government
here for some £500. The offer was declined, and it was snapped up by
Louis Philippe at £1000.* There is a fine replica of this work in Cheshire,

* See note p. 657.

in the gallery of Sir Arthur Aston.* The picture now sold is the identical one which Lord Wellesley, when in Seville, in vain endeavoured to obtain. It is a grand specimen of the master and of the Spanish hidalgo, of sable hair and whisker and costume, and might be taken as the portrait of Cabrera, the renowned guerillero of Don Carlos."

This picture attracted Wilkie's particular attention on his visit to Seville in 1828, and he notices it in his Journal ("Life," iii. 117)—

"'Brackenbury's Murillo'—the man with the dog—is also in the gallery.

"This I saw in the linendraper's (Bravo's) house in Seville, and the expression of the head strikes me as much now as it did then. It seems to see you while you look at it."

Collections—Andrade Family, Seville.
            Antonio Bravo.
            Sir John Brackenbury.
            Louvre, King Louis Philippe, Spanish Gallery, No. 182.
Bought May 14, 1853, No. 328, £1020.
Waagen, *Treasures*, ii. 180.
Viardot, 154.
Stirling, 919-1444.
Curtis, 292, No. 467.
Exhibited—Royal Academy, 1870, No. 86.
Photographed, *Northbrook Gallery*.

* Sold in Sir A. Aston's sale, August 6, 1862, for £472, 10s., and in J. Philip, R.A.'s, sale, May 31, 1867, attributed to Velasquez, for £155, 8s. It was purchased from Messrs. Graves in 1875 by Mr. Cosens of Lewes, who attributes it to Valdez Leal. A copy by Guttierez is in the Academy of San Fernando at Madrid.—*Curtis*.

229   3. ST. THOMAS OF VILLANEUVA.

Canvas.   51¼ × 29½ in.

Figures full length, half life size. The Saint,* in full canonicals
and a white mitre, stands under a vaulted archway giving alms to
a beggar who kneels before him ; an ecclesiastic holds a processional
cross to his right. Behind the beggar are a boy, a man on crutches,
and two women. Another beggar sits on the ground in the foreground to the left, and a boy in rags stands to the right near a
woman with a child in her arms. All of them are looking towards
the Saint. On some clouds above is a figure of Charity, with two
boys at her breast and a third behind. A cathedral is seen in the
background to the left, through the archway. Grey sky.

This picture was painted about 1678 for the chapel of St.
Thomas of Villaneuva in the convent of St. Augustine, outside the
Carmona Gate at Seville. It has always been considered to be one
of the artist's masterpieces, both when at Seville and in the Louvre.
There is another but different representation of the same subject by
Murillo in the Seville Gallery (No. 84),† originally in the Capuchin
convent at Seville.‡ This picture has sometimes been erroneously
described as a study or sketch for the Seville picture, but although
roughly painted, it seems to be quite a finished work, and the composition is different, as well as the attitudes of the figures, from the
Seville picture.

---

* Thomas of Villanueva, son of Alphonso Garcia and Lucia Martinez of Villanueva,
was born in 1488. His family was one of the most ancient of Valencia. When he was
a child he used to give away his food to the poor children, and take off his clothes in
the street, to throw them over those who were in rags. After studying for fourteen
years at Alcala and at Salamanca, he entered the Augustine Order at the age of thirty
on the same day on which Luther publicly renounced the habit of the Order. After
two years' preparation in retirement, he became a distinguished preacher, soon after
Prior of the Augustines at Salamanca, and in 1544 Archbishop of Valencia, where he
devoted two-thirds of the revenues of the see to charity. He died in 1555, and was
declared a "Beato" by Pope Paul V. in 1618.

† See Ford's "Handbook of Spain," 1878. p. 312.

‡ Cean Bermudez, "Diccionario," ii. 62.

Mr. Richard Ford in the *Athenæum*, May 28, 1853, p. 656, calls this picture "the gem of this day's sale—a small but vigorous and sparkling sketch by Murillo in his best manner, long the pride and boast of the Augustine convent of Seville. Surrounded as it was with truculent blood-stained martyrs and black friars, it hung like a rich jewel in an Æthiop's ear. . . . In the treatment of the subject, it differs somewhat from the life-size and magnificent picture painted by the same master for the Capuchin convent, where it was the choice object of Wilkie's veneration, and which still forms one of the pearls of price of the city's museum. It is painted with all the rich and luscious chiaroscuro of Rembrandt, combined with all the national 'borracha' of Spain. It was knocked down, after a spirited competition, for the large sum of £710—not, however, larger than it is worth, being, undoubtedly, one of the finest sketches by Murillo in existence."

Collection—Louvre, King Louis Philippe, Spanish Gallery, No. 171.
Bought May 21, 1853, No. 498, £710.
Viardot, 154. "Une superbe esquisse. Cette composition me semble devoir faire le pendant de *Saint François guérissant un paralytique* que Munich a recueilli dans sa riche Pinacothèque ; c'est du moins la même forme, la même combinaison d'ombre et de jour, la même hauteur d'expression, la même exécution merveilleuse."
Blanc, *Peintres, Ecole Espagnole*, 16.
Mrs. Jameson, *Legends of the Monastic Orders*, 2d edit., London, 1852, 199, 202.
Stirling, 1438.
Curtis, 270, No. 398.
Lithographed by A. Pingon, Paris, 16 × 12 in. On wood in Blanc, p. 11.
Engraved, Jameson, p. 202, and in the *Gazette des Beaux Arts*, April 1875, wrongly called St. Diego.

230   4. ASSUMPTION OF THE VIRGIN.

Copper. Octagon. 13½ × 13½ in.

The twelve Apostles are assembled round a sarcophagus; a woman behind it rests her right hand on a white gravecloth with roses upon it; near her is another woman. On the left, St. Peter kneels holding the keys. Above, the Virgin, with outstretched arms, ascends to heaven, surrounded by eight winged angel heads.

An octagon picture of the same class is in the collection of Lord Lansdowne; it was given to Henry, Marquis of Lansdowne, by Lord Holland.

Collection—Sir Thomas Baring.
Waagen, *Art and Artists*, iii. 41.
   „   *Treasures*, ii. 181.
Stirling, 1410.
Curtis, 130, No. 51.
Exhibited—British Institution, 1840, No. 92.

231   5. LAUGHING BOY.

Panel. 21 × 17½ in.

Half length, life size. A boy in a white shirt, a ragged fur jacket, and a cap crowned with vine leaves, stands turned to the right, and holds before his breast a pipe, with his fingers on the holes.

This picture has also been ascribed to Adrian Brower.

Collections—Sir Thomas Baring. Sold to Mr. Coningham, 1843.
Mr. Coningham.
Bought June 9, 1849, No. 21, £152, 5s.
Passavant, i. 283.
Waagen, *Art and Artists*, iii. 41.
   „   *Treasures*, ii. 181. "The expression of roguery in the eye and mouth is very lively. The influence of Velasquez is seen both in feeling and in the clear reddish tones."
Blanc, 16.
Stirling, 1442.
Curtis, 278, No. 418.
Exhibited—British Institution, 1837, No. 108.

232   6. INFANT SLEEPING.

Canvas.   13½ × 17 in.

A child lies naked on its back on a white cloth spread over a
basket filled with straw.   Dark background.

Collection—Earl of Beverley.
Bought 1851.
Curtis, 278, No. 422.

233   7. HOLY FAMILY.

Canvas.   29 × 23 in.

To the left the Virgin sits in the carpenter's shop with the Child
in her lap.   She wears a violet dress, a grey veil, and a blue
mantle.   A basket with linen and a scarlet cushion are on the
ground at her right.   To the right, Joseph stands at a carpenter's
bench with a compass in his right hand, and at his feet some tools.
Above are three cherubs on clouds descending towards the Child.
In the background a hilly landscape is seen through an open door.

A similar composition is in the collection of the Duke of Devonshire at Chatsworth, executed in the same cool reddish tones.   In
it the head of the Virgin is in profile, the infant Christ is sleeping,
Joseph stands in front cleaving wood, no landscape is seen in the
background, and there are four instead of three cherubs.

Both these pictures were probably painted in the school of
Murillo.

Collection—Sir Thomas Baring.
Waagen, *Art and Artists*, iii. 41.
    „   *Treasures*, ii. 181.
Curtis, 175, No. 142.

MURILLO (ASCRIBED TO).

234   RIPOSO.

Canvas.   54 × 65½ in.

Figures full length, small life size.   In the centre the Virgin,
in a red dress and blue mantle, is seated with the infant Christ
lying before her on a white cloth.   To the left two angel boys stand
looking at the Infant.   Joseph stands behind.   In the foreground
are a bottle and a grey cloth.   Hilly background.

This picture was probably painted in imitation of Murillo.   A
replica attributed to Murillo, but inferior to him, is in the Hermitage Gallery at St. Petersburg; a third, smaller in size, is in
the Glasgow Gallery.   Another, in the Schleissheim Gallery near
Munich, is ascribed to Tobar (Don Alonzo Miguel de Tobar,
1678–1758, who copied many of Murillo's pictures, and was court
painter to Philip V.).

Collections—Lucien Bonaparte.   Sold May 14, 1816, £80(?).
                    Sir Thomas Baring.
Buchanan, ii. 281.
Waagen, *Treasures*, ii. 181.
Curtis, 169, No. 131.
Engraved by Ghigi, *Gallery of Lucien Bonaparte*, London, 1812, No. 100.
    The replica at St. Petersburg is engraved in the *Galerie de l'Hermitage*, by
Labenisky, Petersburg 1805, i., plate 25.
    The replica at Schleissheim is engraved by Piloty, Munich, 1821.

ALONZO SANCHEZ (COELLO), 1515-1590.

235   1. PORTRAIT OF DON DIEGO, SON OF KING
          PHILIP II. OF SPAIN.

Canvas.   42½ × 34¾ in.

Full-length, life-size portrait of a child of about six years of age.
He stands looking to the front; fair hair, blue eyes, in a white
dress richly embroidered with gold.   Round his neck are two gold
chains with a medallion of the Virgin and Child, a crucifix, a heart,
and other ornaments.   In his left hand he holds a hobby-horse, in
his right a toy lance.   Red brick pavement; an open door on the
left, with a balustrade and a view beyond.   Signed on the doorpost

Alfonsus. sanctius. F.
. 1577

and on the top of the picture is the inscription D. diego de Austria.
  This picture, executed in cool greyish tones, and of a firm design,
was apparently painted in imitation of Holbein.   Philip II. married
in 1570 Anna Maria of Austria, second daughter of the Emperor
Maximilian.   She gave birth in 1578 to Philip III., who succeeded
his father.   The boys born previously all died young.*   Don Diego

---

* Histoire Généalogique des Maisons Souveraines de l'Europe, par M. V***. Paris.
1812. Vol. ii., p. 89.

was the fourth. He was born on the 12th of July 1575, and died on the 21st of November 1582. Mr. George Scharf is of opinion that "although in 1577 he was only two years old, the more advanced appearance of the child in the picture is entirely in accordance with the habit of painters to invest their royal and noble infantine sitters with greater maturity."

Collection—Louvre, King Louis Philippe.
Bought May 7, 1853, No. 146, £64.
Waagen, *Galleries*, 96.
Viardot, 154.
Photographed, *Northbrook Gallery*.

236   2. HEAD OF A CHILD.

Canvas. Oval. 11⅞ × 10⅞ in.

Life size, about five years old. Tight cap trimmed with lace. Thick white frock, with a high turned-up collar trimmed with lace. A gold and enamel chain round the neck.

Collection—Mr. Thomas Baring.

SPAGNOLETTO (JUSEPE DE RIBERA), 1588–1656.

237   HOLY FAMILY.

Canvas. 79½ × 60½ in.

Full-length figures, larger than life. To the right the Virgin
sits looking towards the front. Her features are of Spanish type.
Her black hair hangs down her neck. She is dressed in red, with
a blue mantle covering her feet. The infant Christ, with fair hair,
is seated in her arms. A young woman kneels opposite and
devoutly kisses the Child's hand. Behind her stands St. Anne,
holding in her left hand a basket of peaches, and with her right
offering a flower to the Infant. Behind the Virgin stands Joseph.
A basket with red and white clothes stands in the foreground to the
right. Signed on the chair—

Jusepe de Ribera español
accademico R.ͫᵒ
F. 1643

Jusepe de Ribera, called Spagnoletto, of Xátiva, in the kingdom
of Valencia, was a scholar of Francisco Ribalta at Valencia, and
of Caravaggio at Naples. He is the chief representative of the
naturalistic school, which opposed the school of the Carracci. The
pictures which he painted for Spain during his long stay in Italy
are of a pronounced Spanish character. In the year 1630 he was

elected member of the Academy of St. Luc in Rome. The above-described picture is one of the artist's most important works. It not only justifies the high reputation that art history claims for the painter, but it is a standard work, which gives the best basis for a judgment of his principles in art and of his peculiar style.

The kneeling woman has been described to be St. Catherine, but the artist has not given to her any attribute that would justify this name.

Collections—A Gallery in Genoa.
        Lebrun.
        Sir Thomas Baring.
Lebrun, ii. 17. Engraved, No. 128.
Buchanan, ii. 255. "This picture is certainly the finest of this master which is in England, and will rank with any of his works. It is clear and brilliant in tone, and the characters are all graceful and appropriate."
Waagen, *Art and Artists*, iii. 39.
     " *Treasures*, ii. 180.
L. Viardot, 154. "Grande de style, belle d'exécution, parfaitement conservée, et non dans la manière sombre de Caravage, mais tout à fait dans le goût suave de Corrège."
Exhibited—British Institution, 1828, No. 51.
       Royal Academy, 1872, No. 97.

VELASQUEZ (DON DIEGO RODRIGUES DE SILVA),
1599–1660.

238   PHILIP IV. ON HORSEBACK.

Canvas.   23 × 17 in.

The King is in armour, a red scarf round his breast, large black hat with a red feather, a Commander's baton in his right hand. He is mounted on a bay horse with white face and "stockings," and is galloping from left to right.

This picture was described in the Rogers Catalogue as "a finished study for the great picture under which it used to hang in the Retiro." The "great picture" is the life-size portrait of Philip IV. in the Madrid Museum (No. 1066). Don Pedro de Madrazo has lately proved from documents that Velasquez painted it in 1644, in the thirty-ninth year of the King's age, in which year he sat three times for it. It was painted to commemorate his entry into the town of Lérida.

Collection—Mr. Samuel Rogers.
Bought May 3, 1856, No. 693, £215, 5s.
Waagen, Galleries, 96.
Burger, W., W. Stirling, Velasquez et ses Œuvres, Paris, 1865, p. 271, No. 155.
Curtis, 45, No. 98.

VELASQUEZ (ASCRIBED TO).

239 FISH.

Canvas. 11 × 13½ in.

Several small dead fish with a lobster are grouped on a grassy bank; dark background. A hasty but clever sketch. Velasquez "commenced his art career by painting *bodegones*, or objects of still life" (R. Ford in *Athenæum*, May 21, 1853, p. 622).

Collection—Sir Thomas Baring. Bought from Mr. Buchanan.
Exhibited—British Institution, 1845.

ZURBARAN (FRANCESCO DE), 1598–1662.

240 ST. FRANCIS IN MEDITATION.

Canvas. 21½ × 14¾ in.

A small whole-length figure of the Saint, in a brown habit, standing facing the front. The head, which is bent forwards, is covered with a tall pointed hood. In his folded hands he holds a skull.

Collection—Louvre, Louis Philippe.
Bought May 13, 1853, £12.
Waagen, *Galleria*, 96.

FRENCH SCHOOL.

FRANÇOIS BOUCHER, 1704–1768.

241   CUPIDS (a Pair).

Canvas. Oval. 30 × 64 in.

1. A group of five cupids, one with a lighted torch, another writing. Some sculpture in the foreground.

242   2. A group of five cupids playing on musical instruments.

Bought from Mr. Aunoot, 1856.

JACQUES CALLOT, 1593–1635.

243   GIPSIES REMOVING.

Canvas. 11⅞ × 31⅞ in.

The band, passing from left to right, is headed by a man with a musket, followed by a dog. Next come a woman with two children and a man on horseback; then another man with a musket, a woman and two children on a grey horse, and a woman and six children on foot carrying different utensils. A horse and cart laden with furniture follows, and the rear is brought up by a woman on a donkey, with a man by her side. In the distance are some houses.

Collections—Lucca Gallery.
     Sir Thomas Baring.
     Mr. W. Buchanan.
Bought July 4, 1846, No. 7, £30.
Waagen, *Treasures*, ii. 182.
Burger, *Trésors*, 324.
Viardot, 154.

CLAUDE GILLÉE (LORRAINE), 1600-1682.

244   1. JACOB BARGAINING WITH LABAN FOR
HIS DAUGHTER RACHEL.

Copper. 10¾ × 13⅞ in.

In the centre of the foreground, Laban, Leah, Rachel, and Jacob
holding a crook in his left hand, are standing with a flock of sheep
near them. Behind them, on the right, is a clump of trees, and,
farther off, some ruins with a tower. On the left, a river crossed
by a bridge of four arches. Beyond, a town, and in the distance a
bay of the sea with mountains on either side.

A small picture, breathing the coolest morning tones. The figures
by another artist. A larger picture of the same subject is at Petworth ("Liber Veritatis," No. 134).

Collections—M. De la Hante, 1821.
        Prince de Beauveau.
Bought through Mr. Chaplin, 1848.
Liber Veritatis, No. 147, inscribed : "Quadro faict M. Delamart Claudio, 1659."
Smith, viii. 271, No. 147.
Waagen, *Treasures*, 177.

245 2. A SHEPHERD TEACHING A SHEPHERDESS
TO PLAY ON THE PIPE.

Canvas. 20 × 27 in.

In the centre of the foreground a shepherd is sitting on the ground teaching a maiden to play on the pipe. Goats and a cow are grazing near. Beyond, a river flows round a noble clump of trees, which closes the view to the left. To the right, in the mid-distance, are a mill and a round tower; beyond them, high rocks, from which a stream falls in a cascade. In the distance are mountains, and at their foot a town is just visible.

A beautiful and carefully-executed work of the artist's middle period. The evening light admirably rendered.

Painted for Signor Piretti.

Collections—Mr. John Glover. Sold in 1830 for £736 to Mr. Stanley.
     Mr. John Smith.
     Sir Thomas Baring.
Liber Veritatis, No. 123, inscribed : " Claudio f. v. R. G. Perette." *
Smith, viii. 259, No. 123 ; ix. 808, No. 16.
Waagen, *Treasures*, ii. 177.
Exhibited—Royal Academy, 1880, No. 85.

---

* The inscriptions are taken from the original of the " Liber Veritatis " at Chatsworth. Claude was not particular in his spelling ; for instance, in the list appended to the book he spells the name " Peretta."—N.

246   3. A SHEPHERD PLAYING ON A PIPE.

Canvas.   20¾ × 27 in.

A landscape with trees on the left, near which, in the immediate foreground, is a shepherd in blue, piping, seated on a mound.   To the right, goats at rest or browsing, and, farther off, a man driving some cattle into a woody dell, above which, on the extreme right, in the middle distance, rises a rocky hill, the steep sides of which are clothed with bushy trees, while the summit is crowned by a castle.   On a winding river, to the left, is a boat; in the distance, a four-arched bridge; beyond it, the mouth of a river with a mountain and a town. Blue sky with setting sun.

Collections—Lord Kinnaird. Sold for £1000 to Mr. Glover.
         Mr. John Glover. Bought in in 1830 at £735.
         Mr. John Smith.
         Sir Thomas Baring. Bought with the preceding from Mr. Smith.
Liber Veritatis, No. 172, inscribed: " 1667 A Roma Claudio Gillæ inventor fecit per Palerma."
Smith, viii. 288, No. 172 ; ix. 808, No. 17.
Waagen, *Treasures*, ii. 177.
Engraved by Dubourg.
Exhibited—Royal Academy, 1889, No. 88.

247   4. WATERFALL.

Canvas.   19¼ × 15 in.

On the left is a rocky bank covered with trees with a waterfall in front of it. On the right, on the bank in the foreground, is a shepherd leaning upon his staff, with two goats, a sheep, and a cow near him. Hills in the distance.

This picture is very like the drawing in the " Liber Veritatis," vol. iii., No. 22, both in the character of the scenery and the attitude of the shepherd.

Collection—Earl of Beverley.
Bought in 1851.
Smith, viii. 379, No. 411.

248   5. THE ARTIST STUDYING FROM NATURE.

Canvas.   29½ × 38 in.

A sea-coast view at the mouth of the Tiber, in the warmest glow of
evening sunshine. In the foreground are the artist, sketching, and
two other persons; beyond them a clump of trees, and, on the right,
a gateway flanked by two towers, part of the fortifications of the
town of Ostia, towards which peasants and others are wending their
way. On the left, a boat is discharging its cargo. In the distance,
on the other side of the bay, are buildings with mountains (added
from fancy) beyond. On the ground, near the artist, are a couple of
carved capitals and some fragments. Signed and dated Rome, 1674.*
There is a picture of the same subject, but rather longer, at
Burleigh.

Collections—A Collection of pictures imported from the Continent by Mr. La
        Fontaine. Sold June 13, 1807, No. 40, £1995.
        Sir Thomas Baring.
Liber Veritatis, No. 44, inscribed : "Quadro faict per M. Perochat. Claudio
fecit."
Smith, viii. 308, No. 384.
Waagen, Treasures, ii. 177.
Exhibited—Manchester, 1857, No. 819, and a sketch, No. 180. "Civita Vecchia
and two ships—Rev. Dr. Wellesley, from the De Fries, Laurence, and Eslaile
Collections."

* NOTE.—The letters of the signature and the figures of the date are not very dis-
tinct.

249   6. CLAUDE'S FAVOURITE MILL.

Canvas. 29 × 38½ in.

On the right, steep wooded hills extend half across the picture.
with streams of water and some buildings. On the left, in the middle
distance, there is a river crossed by a bridge of six arches. In the
foreground is a cluster of high trees, and on the extreme left more
trees, beneath the shade of which a shepherd in red and a shepherdess
in blue are sitting, their goats and cows feeding near them. In the
distance, mountains of tender blue.

> Collections—Sold June 13, 1807, No. 41, "Le Moulin favori," £840, to Mr.
>   Clifford.
>   Sir Thomas Baring.
> Smith, viii. 368, No. 385.
> Waagen, *Treasures*, ii. 177.

250   7. ASCANIUS SHOOTING AT SILVIA'S
STAG.

Canvas. 47 × 59¼ in.

A hilly country near the sea, with a river running between high
banks. On the left is the portico (with four columns) of a temple
in ruins. Ascanius, in front of it, is in the act of shooting at
the stag, which stands on a wooded bank opposite ; behind him are
six followers and three hounds. On the heights behind the temple
are trees and buildings ; in the background is a bridge with
peasants and donkeys crossing it. On the right are cliffs crowned
by buildings, and in the centre, in the distance, the sea-shore.

In the front is an inscription, now hardly legible, but which
appears to run thus : "A Roma 1678. Come Ascanio asetta il
cervo di Silvia figliuola di Tirro, Lib. 7" (Virgil, Æneis, vii.
483, &c.). On the back of the picture is the inscription, "Quadro
per l'Illma et excell^{ma} Sig. Contestabile Colonna questo di 5 Ottobre
1681."

A sketch of the subject, but without the ruined temple and with some other variations, with the date 1678, is in the " Liber Veritatis," iii. 98. Smith, viii. 383, identifies this picture with the sketch. An original drawing of the picture, dated 1682, from the collection of Lord Palmerston, is also in Lord Northbrook's possession.

Collections—Colonna Palace, Catalogue, No. 153.
              Mr. W. Young Ottley, May 16, 1801, No. 31.
              Mr. Walsh Porter. Sold April 14, 1810, No. 48, £630, to Mr.
                  Webster.
              A Collection. Sold May 6, 1826, No. 9, £262, 10s., to Mr. Peacock.
              Sir Thomas Baring.
Smith, viii. 383, No. 293.
Waagen, *Art and Artists*, iii. 40.
   ,,   *Treasures*, 177. "Said to be the last large picture by the master."
Engraved in reverse by Pond.

Dr. Waagen (*Treasures*, ii. 177) gives the following description of six of the Claudes :—

" In the six pictures here preserved we trace the master from his earlier to his later period.

(No. 0.) " 1. A landscape, with a bridge in the middle ground ; in front, a shepherd and shepherdess ; on the left, houses in the wood ; mountains of tender blue in the distance. The juicy green of the trees, and the conception and treatment of this beautiful picture, indicate the master's earlier period ; the keeping is somewhat disturbed, however, by the after darkening of the middle ground.

(No. 1.) " 2. A small picture with the subject of Laban, Jacob, Rachel and Leah ; breathing the coolest morning tones. Of a rather later period.

(No. 6.) " 3. A sea-coast, in the warmest glow of sunshine. In the foreground are the artist drawing, and two other persons. This careful and spirited picture, of excellent body, is of his best time ; of the same period as the view of the Campo Vaccino in the Louvre, which was ruined in 1851.

(No. 2.) " 4. A landscape with trees and water ; in front a shepherd piping. A charming picture, of his middle time.

(No. 3.) " 5. The setting sun, the rays of which are seen, is pouring its light in the tenderest gradations upon every object. In front a shepherd piping, and his flock. This beautiful and carefully-carried-out work is also of the middle time.

(No. 7.) " 6. In strong contrast to the foregoing is the picture purchased by Mr. Ottley from the Colonna Palace, with the subject of Æneas, with several companions, shooting at a stag—said to be the last large picture by the master. The cool, fresh tones of early morning and the beautiful lines of the landscape show the great painter, though the cold green of the trees and the slight treatment betray a manifest decline. Also the figures are so stiff, and so tall in proportion to the landscape, that a child might have painted them as well."

CLAUDE GILLÉE (ASCRIBED TO).

251   LANDSCAPE, WITH FIGURES.

Canvas.   21½ × 36¾ in.

A wooded landscape with a river bounded by hills. In the centre of the foreground, a group of three shepherds in conversation; to the right, a fourth seated, and a fifth following a cow which is entering a wood on the extreme left. Beyond these, cows and goats reposing or watering; a ferryboat pushing off with four figures and a mule in it. On the left, houses and trees with a round tower above. In the distance, hills. Blue evening sky with a few clouds.

Attributed by Waagen to Agostino Tassi. Claude, though Tassi's pupil, was not indebted to him for his style of composition, which was entirely original. This landscape, being altogether in Claude's manner, though inferior to his authentic pictures, must be the work of a contemporary, or more probably of a later imitator.

Collection—Sir Thomas Baring.
Waagen, *Treasures*, ii. 177.

GASPAR DUGHET, CALLED GASPAR POUSSIN,
1613–1675.

252   1. LANDSCAPE.

Canvas.   47 × 66 in.

A forest with an open glade in the centre, in which is a stream with a waterfall. In the foreground, a group of four figures at rest, two with urns. In the mid-distance, a woman seated playing a tambourine, and, on the farther side of the stream, a youth running followed by a hound. Blue sky with clouds.

Collection—Sir Thomas Baring.

253   2. LANDSCAPE, WITH FIGURES.

Canvas.   17⅛ × 13⅞ in.

In the foreground are two figures resting.   On the left, a tree.
On the right, a lofty mountain.   In the background, a stream and
distant hills.

Collection—Sir Thomas Baring.

254   3. THE ARCH.

Panel.   17½ × 23⅞ in.

A winding road leads up from the left foreground to a natural
arch, formed by rocks overgrown with shrubs, showing a view
beyond.   On the road are a man with a stick and his dog, and
at the foot of a tree, to the right, a man lying down.   In the
background, a mountain.

Collections—Sir H. C. Englefield.   Sold, March 8, 1823, No. 64, £30, 18s., to
          Mr. Norton.
          Colonel Baillie.   Sold, March 6, 1824, No. 67, £40, 19s.
Bought from Mr. Farrer, 1849.
Waagen, *Treasures*, ii. 177.   "A picture of great charm, both in point of poetic
composition and transparent colouring."
Exhibited—Royal Academy, 1872, No. 102.

255   4. LANDSCAPE.

Canvas.   27¾ × 37½ in.

In the foreground, on either side, trees.   On the right, a shepherd and a flock of sheep; in the centre, a youth and a maiden
resting; on the left, a man lying down, and farther off, another
advancing towards the centre.   In the background, on the left, a
castle and a hill beyond; on the right, an extensive distant view.

Collection—Sir Thomas Baring.

JEAN BAPTISTE GREUZE, 1726-1805.

256   ### HEAD OF A GIRL.

Canvas. 18 × 14½ in.

Life size. Turned to the right. A muslin kerchief round the head. Grey dress loosely fastened round the shoulders.

Bought from Colonel Temple, 1859.

SCHOOL OF GREUZE.

257   ### HEAD OF A GIRL.

Canvas. 17⅞ × 14⅞ in.

Life size. Three-quarters face looking down to the left. A light blue ribbon round the head. Square-cut frock. Muslin scarf round the shoulders.

Collection—Mr. Thomas Baring.

PIERRE MIGNARD, 1610-1695.

258   ### MADAME DE LA VALLIÈRE.

Canvas. 38 × 29½ in.

Half length, life size. Sitting down, in a blue silk dress, with pearls in her hair. Her left elbow rests on a table; in her left hand she holds a string of pearls, which is broken. Above, on the left, a curtain looped up.

Collection—Mr. Ralph Bernal.
Bought March 10, 1855, No. 703, £81, 18s.

CLEMENT MOREAU.

259   SUPPER PARTY.

Panel. $8\frac{1}{2} \times 6\frac{3}{4}$ in.

A party of four at dessert by candlelight. On the table a group of the Three Graces supporting a tazza on which is a pineapple. One lady is engaging a gentleman to drink, the other is reading a letter, which the second gentleman is trying to get possession of by passing his arm behind her.

Bought from Mr. Pearce, 1866.

——— ——

CLAUD JOSEPH VERNET, 1714-1789.

260   1. VIEW NEAR NAPLES.

View on the coast in the environs of Naples, with ruins and buildings on the heights above; boats on the shore. The figures, painted with good taste, and placed with propriety, tend much to enliven the picture.

Collections—M. de Calonne, Paris. Sold March 27, 1795, No. 72, £165.
       Sir Francis Baring.
       Sir Thomas Baring. Sold June 3, 1848, No. 91, £30, 9s.
       Sir Francis T. Baring (Lord Northbrook).
Buchanan, i. 239.

261   2. BALÆ.

Canvas. 47 × 66 in.

View on the shore, near Baiæ, with the Temple of Venus and nymphs bathing.

Collections—M. de Calonne, Paris. Sold March 27, 1795, No. 73, £150.
         Sir Francis Baring.
         Sir Thomas Baring. Sold June 3, 1848, No, 92, £26, 5s.
         Sir Francis T. Baring (Lord Northbrook).
Buchanan, i. 239.

PIERRE ALEXANDRE WILLE, 1748–

262   DEDICACE D'UN POËME EPIQUE.

Canvas. 23¾ × 19 in.

On the right, a lady in a pink dress is sitting in an arm-chair, holding a cup and saucer in her left hand and a spoon in her right ; her left arm rests on a small table, on which is a coffee-pot. At her side stands her maid. In front, a poet is reciting from a book, the title-page of which bears :

LA BAGATELLE

POEME

en xxx chants

Dedié a Mademoiselle

· · · · · · · · · · · · · · ·

A PARIS

Out of his pocket protrude some papers, one of which is inscribed : "Vers à Mimy petit chien de Mademoiselle De * * *." In the background a curtained bed. In the foreground, on the right, a basket with knitting, &c. Signed : P. A WILLE, 1780, No. 53.

Collection—Mr. Thomas Baring.
Engraved by A. F. Dennel.

APPENDIX.

I.

CATALOGUE OF THE VERSTOLK GALLERY.

THE collection of Baron Verstolk van Soelen consisted of 100 pictures. One was sold to the King of Holland, and the remainder were divided between the three purchasers, Mr. Baring, Mr. Jones Loyd, and Mr. Humphrey Mildmay, and Mr. Chaplin through whom the purchase was made. The following catalogue has been compiled from the list furnished by Mr. Brondgeest, who had bought many of Baron Verstolk's pictures for him and who acted for his estate. Some descriptions of the pictures taken from other lists have been added, as well as the references to Smith's *Catalogue Raisonné* for the pictures which are not now in my collection. At the end of Mr. Brondgeest's list is the following certificate in his handwriting :—

" I hereby certify that the pictures described in this list are the whole of the collection of the late Baron Verstolk van Soelen, with the exception of two family pictures not included, agreeable to the arrangement made with Mr. Chaplin.

" A. BRONDGEEST.

" HAGUE, *June* 29, 1846."

The names of the purchasers are taken from lists made at the time; and, as the value of high-class pictures is a matter of some interest, I append the figures of the transaction. The total sum paid for the collection was £26,231. Mr. Baring bought 43 pictures for £12,472, Mr. Jones Loyd 10 for £8116, Mr. Mildmay 20 for £4543, and Mr. Chaplin 26 for £1100.—(*N.*)

No.	Name.		Description.
1	Asselyn, J.	.	An Italian landscape, with figures and cattle.
2	Backhuisen, L. .	.	Various shipping in an agitated water.
3	Bega, C. . .	.	Interior—an alchymist in study.
4	Berchem, N. .	.	A landscape—a woman carrying a lamb—cows and sheep, &c.
5	Berkheyde, G. .	.	View of the Stadthouse in Haarlem.
6	Do.	.	View in Haarlem.
7	Bol, F.	.	A lady dressing before a glass, a gentleman looking on.
8	Do.	.	A group of females, one being crowned with flowers.
9	Do. . .	.	Portrait of Admiral de Ruyter.
10	Brekelencamp, Q.	.	An interior—an old woman with a boy.
11	Cuyp, A. . .	.	A view on a river—various shipping.
12	De Heem, J. .	.	A vase with fruit, a bottle with flowers.
13	De Hoogh, P. .	.	An interior—a woman with a loaf of bread.
14	De Witte, E. .	.	Interior—effect of sunlight—lady playing on the clavecin.
15 16	Do. Do.	}	A pair of interiors of churches.
17	Du Jardin, K. .	.	A landscape, with a man and two sheep.
18	Dusart, C.	.	An interior of a cottage—a woman with a child.
19	Hackaert, J. .	.	A landscape, with cattle. The figures by A. Van de Velde.
20	Do.	.	A view in the wood at the Hague. Figures by A. Van de Velde.

Purchaser.	Present Possessor.	Remarks.
Baring.	Northbrook, No. 28.	
Mildmay.	Mr. H. Bingham Mildmay.	Smith, VI. No. 95.
Chaplin.	......	"Cabane avec des paysans."
Mildmay.	Mr. H. Bingham Mildmay.	Smith, V. No. 56.
Baring.	Northbrook, No. 32.	
Chaplin.	......	"Vue d'une partie de la grande église à Haarlem."
Baring.	Northbrook, No. 34.	
Do.	Do. No. 35.	"Diane et ses nymphes."
Do.	Do. No. 36.	
Do.	......	No record of this picture.
Do.	Northbrook, No. 44.	
Chaplin.	......	
Mildmay.	Mr. H. Bingham Mildmay.	Smith, IV. No. 54
Do.	Do.	This picture is ascribed to N. Maas in some of the lists.
Baring.	Northbrook, Nos. 51 and 52.	
Mildmay.	Mr. H. Bingham Mildmay.	Smith, Supplement No. 19.
Baring.	Northbrook, No. 55.	
Do.		"Vue en Italie richement ornée de figures." Smith, VI. No. 12. Given away by Mr. Baring.
Jones Loyd.	Lord Wantage, Carlton Terrace. Catalogue No. 71.	"Avec un départ pour la chasse des personnages de la cour de Guillaume II."

No.	Name.	Description.
21	Hobbema, M. . .	An overshot mill by a cottage, a church in the distance.
22	Do. .	A view in Amsterdam, with the herring-packers' tower.
23	Koninck, P.	A grand landscape. Figures by A. Van de Velde.
24	Koninck, S. .	An old man's head.
25	Lingelbach, J. . .	An Italian landscape—figures dancing.
26	Do. .	An Italian landscape—river, boats, figures.
27	Do. .	Travellers and horses at an inn-door.
28	Do. .	View of a market in Rome—numerous figures.
29	Maas, N. . .	A grand landscape, with a hunting-party, in which is introduced the portrait of William III.
30	Metsu, G. . .	A gentleman intruding himself into a lady's chamber.
31	Do. . .	A portrait of himself, with a pipe.
32	Mignon, A. .	Fruit—still life—a bird's nest.
33 34	Musscher . Do. .	Two interiors—one a lady with her servant, the other a man with a duck.
35	Do. .	Portrait of William Van de Velde.
36	Pynacker, A. .	A large grand landscape—figures, cattle, wooden bridge.
37	Do. .	An Italian landscape—a bridge, with a river, boats, &c.
38	Do. .	Upright landscape, with figures.
39	Rembrandt .	Portrait of an old lady (his grandmother).

Purchaser.	Present Possessor.	Remarks.
Jones Loyd.	Lord Wantage, Carlton Terrace. Catalogue No. 7.	Smith, VI. No. 67.
Mildmay.	Mr. H. Bingham Mildmay.	Smith, VI. No. 28.
Baring.	Northbrook, No. 64.	"Un paysage en Gueldre."
Do.	Do. No. 65.	
Do.	Do. No. 69.	"Fête champêtre dans les environs de Rome."
Mildmay.	Mr. H. Bingham Mildmay.	
Do.	Do.	
Chaplin.		
King of Holland.		
Baring.	Northbrook, No. 74.	"La surprise."
Do.	Do. No. 75.	
Chaplin.		
Do.		
Baring.	Northbrook, No. 136.	
Do.	-	Smith, VI. No. 39. Sold in 1849 to Lord C. Townshend. Sold in 1851 to Mr. Rutley for £270.
Jones Loyd.	Lord Wantage, Carlton Terrace. Catalogue No. 14.	Smith, Supplement No. 8.
Chaplin.	......	
Jones Loyd.	Lord Wantage, Carlton Terrace. Catalogue No. 73.	Smith, VII. No. 516.

No.	Name.	Description.
40	Rembrandt . .	Portrait of an old man with a velvet cap.
41	Rombonts, P. . .	A landscape, with figures.
42	Romeyn . . .	A landscape, with cattle.
43 44	Ruisdael, J. . Do. .	A view of Schoveningen Beach—figures, boats, &c.—a pair.
45	Do. .	A grand rocky landscape, with waterfall.
46	Do. .	A landscape, with a cornfield.
47 48	Saftleven, H. . Do.	A pair of river views—boats, figures, &c.
49 50	Schalken, G. Do.	Pair of portraits, a lady and a gentleman.
51	Shillinks . .	A winter piece, with snow, figures, &c.
52	Steen, J. . .	A portrait of himself playing the guitar.
53	Do. .	A doctor writing a prescription, a woman in bed.
54	Do.	Schoolmaster asleep, boys playing.
55	Do.	Jan Steen going to be married—numerous figures.
56	Do.	An interior—a jovial party merrymaking.
57	Do.	An interior—candlelight, figures playing cards, &c.
58 59	Terburgh, G. . Do. .	A pair—a lady drinking a glass of wine, another writing.
60	Van de Capelle, J. .	Still water, with passage-boat, &c.
61	Do. . .	View on a river—various shipping, moving water.

Purchaser.	Present Possessor.	Remarks.
Baring.	Northbrook, No. 85.	
Do.	......	Sold to Mr. Chaplin 1846.
Mildmay.	Mr. H. Bingham Mildmay.	
Do.	Do.	Smith, VI. Nos. 19 and 20. Engraved in the Choiseul Gallery, Nos. 117 and 118.
Jones Loyd.	Lord Wantage, Carlton Terrace. Catalogue No. 3.	Smith, VI. No. 129.
Chaplin.		Smith, Supplement No. 80.
Do.		
Baring.	Northbrook, No. 95.	Portrait of a lady. Smith, Supplement No. 10. Sold to Mr. Chaplin 1846.
Do.	......	Sold to Mr. Chaplin 1846.
Do.	Northbrook, No. 97.	
Do.	Do. No. 98.	
Do.	Do. No. 99.	
Do.	Baron A. de Rothschild. Catalogue No. 28.	Smith, IV. No. 139.
Jones Loyd.	Lord Wantage, Carlton Terrace. Catalogue No. 20.	" Joueur de cornemuse." " Celebrating Twelfth Night." " St. Nicholas' Day." Smith, IV. No. 51.
Mildmay.	Mr. H. Bingham Mildmay.	Smith, Supplement No. 86.
Baring.	Northbrook, Nos. 113 and 114.	
Mildmay.	Mr. H. Bingham Mildmay.	
Chaplin.	......	

No.	Name.		Description.
62	Van de Velde, A.	.	A hunting-party preparing to start.
63	Do.	.	A hunting-party in a landscape, white horse, &c.
64	Do.	.	A landscape, with cows, sheep, and figures.
65	Van de Velde, W.	.	Still water, with various shipping.
66	Do.	.	Still water—a smaller picture, a man-of-war at anchor in the distance.
67	Van den Eeckhout	.	A pleasure-party taking refreshments.
68	Van der Hagen	.	A landscape. Figures by A. Van de Velde.
69	Van der Helst	.	A small portrait of a gentleman.
70	Van der Heyde	.	A landscape, with a bridge, castle, &c.
71	Do.	.	A view in a town. Figures by A. Van de Velde.
72 73	Van der Neer, A. Do.	}	A pair—evening and morning.
74	Do.	.	A landscape—men cutting wood, fishermen with nets.
75	Do.	.	A landscape, cows and figures in the foreground.
76	Do.	.	A landscape by moonlight.
77	Do.	.	A landscape—winter, with snow.
78 79	Van Hughtenburg Do.	}	A pair of battles.
80	Van Kessel, A.	.	Landscape, with a bleaching-ground.
81	Van Tol, D.	.	A girl at a window gathering a pink. After G. Dow.

Purchaser.	Present Possessor.	Remarks.
Baring.	Baron A. de Rothschild. Catalogue No. 35.	"Chasse royale." Smith, V. No. 27. Exchanged in 1881.
Do.		"Rendezvous de chasse." Smith, V. No. 32. Sold in 1885.
Mildmay.	Mr. H. Bingham Mildmay.	Smith, V. No. 12.
Jones Loyd.	Lord Wantage, Carlton Terrace. Catalogue No. 30.	Smith, VI. No. 126.
Mildmay.	Mr. H. Bingham Mildmay.	
Chaplin.		"Faisant de la musique."
Do.		"Entrée d'un bois avec des chasseurs."
Do.		
Do.	......	
Baring.	Northbrook, No. 123.	
Do.	Northbrook, Nos. 124 and 125.	
Jones Loyd	Lord Wantage, Carlton Terrace. Catalogue No. 15.	
Do.	Do. do. No. 13.	
Mildmay.	Mr. H. Bingham Mildmay.	
Chaplin.	......	"Avec des patineurs."
Do.		
Baring.	Mr. W. Baring, Norman Court.	"Vue dans les environs de Haarlem." Given to him 1877.
Do.	Northbrook, No. 141.	

No.	Name.	Description.
82	Van Ostade, A. .	An interior—three Boors smoking and drinking.
83	Van Vliet, J. .	Interior of the church at Delft.
84	Verboom, A. .	A landscape. Figures by A. Van de Velde.
85	Do. .	A grand landscape—hunting. Figures by Lingelbach.
86	Victor, J. .	A landscape—figures in a boat, &c.
87	Do. .	A landscape, with a peddller selling his wares.
88	Wouverman, Peter .	A castle—figures preparing for the chase.
89	Wouverman, Philip .	Horse-fair.
90	Do. .	Horses leading to water.
91	Do. .	Plundering prisoners after battle.
92	Do. .	A battle—a building on fire.
93	Do. .	Small landscape, with hawking party.
94	Wynants, J. .	A grand landscape—bandits attacking a traveller.
95	Do. .	A landscape. Figures by A. Van de Velde.
96	Wyk, T. .	Italian landscape, with figures—a fountain.

MODERN PICTURES.

No.	Name.	Description.
97	Hulswit, J. .	A landscape, with cottage, figures, &c.
98	Koeckkoek, J. .	A winter piece, with snow.
99	Do. .	A landscape, with hunting-party.
100	Schotel, J. C. .	A ship in a storm.

Purchaser.	Present Possessor.	Remarks.
Baring.		Smith, I. No. 207, and Supplement No. 107. Exchanged with Mr. Buchanan.
Do.	Northbrook, No. 142.	
Do.	Do. No. 143.	
Chaplin.		
Do.		
Do.		
Do.	......	
Baring.	Northbrook, No. 147.	
Do.	Baron A. de Rothschild. Catalogue No. 40.	Smith, I. No. 453 (1), Supplement No. 217. Exchanged 1881.
Do.		Smith, Supplement No. 96. Exchanged with Mr. Smith 1847.
Mildmay.	Mr. H. Bingham Mildmay.	Smith, I. No. 455, and Supplement No. 97.
Do.	Do.	
Do.	Do.	Figures by P. Wouverman. Smith, VI. No. 81, and Supplement No. 17.
Jones Loyd.	Lord Wantage, Lockinge. Catalogue No. 10.	Smith, VI. No. 133.
Chaplin.	......	
Baring.		Sold 1847.
Mildmay.		
Chaplin.	......	
Do.	......	

II.

PICTURES BOUGHT BY SIR THOMAS BARING FROM THE LE BRUN GALLERY.

The following account of the Le Brun Collection is given by Mr. Buchanan:[1]—

" In the year 1810 Monsieur Le Brun exhibited in Paris a large collection of pictures which he had formed in journeys made in Spain and Italy during the years 1807 and 1808. The times were not favourable in Paris for a sale of these objects, and a great many of them were withdrawn or purchased by the proprietor himself for the purpose of being consigned to Mr. Harris, of Bond Street, who received a large proportion of those objects which appear in the original catalogue published at Paris.

" Monsieur Le Brun, in publishing a catalogue of that collection, also gave a small volume of etchings after some of the leading pictures which it contained."

Name.	Le Brun.		Present Possessor and Remarks.
	Page	Plate	
Bellini, G. . . . Virgin and Child.	i. 29.	XV.	Northbrook, No. 154.
Bolognese . Landscape.	i. 125.	CXVI.	Mr.Wm. Baring, Norman Court; given to him, 1877.
Carracci, An. . . Virgin and Child.	i. 99.	LXXIX.	Mr. Holford; sold to him, 1843.
Carracci, L. . . Entombment.	i. 94.	LXXII.	Northbrook, No. 162.
Do. . Bathsheba.	i. 94.	LXXIII.	Do. No. 161.

[1] " Memoirs of Painting," ii. 251.

Name.	Le Brun.		Present Possessor and Remarks
	Page	Plate	
Cortona, P. da St. Jerome.	i. 24.	XI.	Northbrook, No. 170.
Do. Adoration of the Shepherds.	i. 24.	X.	Do. No. 172.
Dolci, C. Christ with the Cross	i. 26.	XIV.	Do. No. 177.
Lionardo da Vinci. Head of Christ.	i. 6.	II.	Do. No. 189.
Maznell, G. Woman with a Lamp.	i. 90.	LXIX.	Destroyed.
Murillo, B. Immaculate Conception.	ii. 25.	CXXXIV.	Northbrook, No. 227.
Do. St. John and the Lamb.	ii. 25.	CXXXV.	Sold by Sir Thomas Baring.
Piombo, S. del Holy Family.	i. 37.	XXI.	Northbrook, No. 201.
Ricci, S.	i. 118.	CV.	Mr. Wm. Baring, Norman Court; given to him, 1877; ascribed by Le Brun to Domenichino.
Rosa, J. Landscape.	ii. 8.	CXXI.	Northbrook, No. 207.
Do. St. John Preaching.	ii. 8.	CXXIII.	Do. No. 208.
Sarto, A. del. Portrait.	i. 65.	XL.	Do. No. 211. Ascribed by Le Brun to Raphael.
Sebedone Riposo.	i. 101.	LXXXIV.	Northbrook, No. 215.
Spagnoletto. Holy Family.	ii. 17.	CXXVIII.	Do. No. 237.
Titian The Falconer.	i. 34.	XVIII.	Mr. Holford; sold to him, 1843.
Do. Portrait.	i. 34.	XVII.	Do. do.
Do. Landscape—Holy Family.	i. 34.	XVI.	Sold to the late Lord Taunton, 1843; now in the possession of the Hon. Mrs. Stanley, Quantock Lodge.
Vaga, P. del. Holy Family.	i. 60.	XLI.	Northbrook, No. 219. Ascribed by Le Brun to Giulio Romano.
Velasquez	ii. 23.	CXXIX.	Mr. Holford; sold to him, 1843.

APPENDIX.

III.

WORKS REFERRED TO IN THE CATALOGUE.

BUCHANAN.—Memoirs of Painting. With a Chronological History of the Importation of Pictures by the Great Masters into England since the French Revolution. By W. Buchanan, Esq. 2 vols. 8vo. London. Ackermann. 1824.

BÜRGER.—Trésors d'Art en Angleterre. Par W. Bürger. Bruxelles. 1860.

CROWE and CAVALCASELLE.—History of Painting in Italy. 3 vols. 8vo. London. Murray. 1846.

CURTIS.—Velasquez and Murillo. A Descriptive and Historical Catalogue. By Charles B. Curtis, M.A. New York. J. W. Bouton. 1883.

KUGLER (Handbook).—Handbook of Painting. The German, Flemish, and Dutch Schools, based on the Handbook of Kugler; remodelled by the late Prof. Dr. Waagen. A new edition, thoroughly revised, and in part rewritten, by J. A. Crowe. In two parts. London. Murray. 1874.

KUGLER (Handbook). Layard.—Handbook of Painting. The Italian Schools, based on the Handbook of Kugler, originally edited by Sir Charles Eastlake, P.R.A. Fifth edition, thoroughly revised, and in part rewritten, by Austin Henry Layard, G.C.B. In two parts. London. Murray. 1887.

LE BRUN.—Recueil de Gravures au trait, à l'eau forte et ombrées, d'après un choix de tableaux de toutes les écoles, recueillis dans un voyage fait en Espagne, au Midi de la France et en Italie dans les années 1807 et 1808. Par M. Le Brun, Peintre, &c. 2 vols. 8vo. Paris. Didot Jeune. 1809.

NIEUWENHUYS.—A Review of the Lives and Works of some of the most Eminent Painters, with Remarks on the Opinions and Statements of Former Writers. By C. J. Nieuwenhuys. London. Henry Hooper. 1834.

NORTHBROOK GALLERY.—The Northbrook Gallery. An Illustrated Descriptive and Historic Account of the Collection of the Earl of Northbrook, G.C.S.I. Edited by Lord Ronald Gower, F.S.A. London. Sampson Low & Co. 1885.

PASSAVANT.—Johann David Passavant. Tour of a German Artist in England, with Notices of Private Galleries, and Remarks on the State of Art. 2 vols. 12mo. London. 1836.

SMITH.—A Catalogue Raisonné of the Works of the most Eminent Dutch, Flemish, and French Painters, &c. By John Smith, Dealer in Pictures, late of Great Marlborough Street. 9 vols. 8vo. London. Smith & Son. 1829, &c.

STIRLING.—Annals of the Artists of Spain. By William Stirling, M.A. 3 vols. 8vo. London. Olivier. 1848.

WAAGEN (Art and Artists).—Works of Art and Artists in England. By G. F. Waagen, Director of the Royal Gallery at Berlin. 3 vols. sm. 8vo. London. Murray. 1838.

WAAGEN (Treasures).—Treasures of Art in Great Britain. Being an Account of the Chief Collections of Paintings, described by Dr. Waagen, Director of the Royal Gallery of Pictures, Berlin. 3 vols. 8vo. London. Murray. 1854.

WAAGEN (Galleries).—Galleries and Cabinets of Art in Great Britain. Being an Account of more than Forty Collections of Paintings, &c., visited in 1854 and 1856, and now for the first time described. By Dr. Waagen, &c. Forming a supplemental volume to the "Treasures of Art." London. Murray. 1857.

VIARDOT. — Louis Viardot. Les Musées d'Angleterre, de Belgique, de Hollande et de Russie. Third edition. Paris. Hachette & Co. 1860.

ADDITIONAL NOTES.

Page 119.—L. Carracci, Pieta. The figure of Christ is very like that of the large Pieta ascribed to A. Carracci, engraved in *Musée Napoléon*, Vol. iii., No. 181. There is a similar composition in the Doria Gallery, Rome.

Page 130.—Domenichino, Ripose. A picture of the same class, both as to size and composition, called "La Vierge à la Coquille," is in the Louvre, engraved in *Musée Napoléon*, Vol. ii., No. 84.

Page 130.—B. Luini, Holy Family. A copy of this picture is in the Brera Gallery at Milan, Galleria Oggioni, No. 76.

Page 176, line 28.—The engravings are of the picture in the Gallery of Seville.

INDEX.

(215)

INDEX.

INDEX.

INDEX.

INDEX.

(219)

INDEX.

INDEX.

(221)

INDEX.